Covert Messages

Hidden Plans of an Alien Intelligence Network

Rodney Jensen

Rodney Jensen Books

First published in Australia in 2021

Rodney Jensen Books
http://www.rodneyjensenbooks.com/

PO Box 357 St Leonards NSW 1590 Australia

ISBN 978-0-9941668-8-3

CiPcatalogue record for this book is available from the National Library of Australia.

Cover design - Rockingbook Covers

Dedication

To all readers whose imaginations are unconstrained by the boundaries of our world, to those who recognize the inconceivable span of our universe in time and space, and to those who see the probability that intelligence and consciousness are not unique to this planet.

"I think it very likely - in fact inevitable - that biological intelligence is only a transitory phenomenon, a fleeting phase in the evolution of intelligence in the universe. If we ever encounter extraterrestrial intelligence, I believe it is overwhelmingly likely to be post-biological in nature..."

Paul Davies, 'The Eerie Silence', published by Penguin 2011

Be the first to hear all about Rodney Jensen's new books - the **Covert Trilogy** and others.

Sign up to RodneyJensenBooks Mailing List

ahttps://www.subscribepage.com/y4a2w9_copy2

PROLOGUE

As the bio-scientists were quietly going about their experiments in the top security lab, they were jolted into urgent escape mode by the penetrating and pulsating rasp of an emergency siren. In their anxiety to retreat the research staff in full PPE (Personal Protective Equipment) had torn off the air hoses tying them to their work stations and run to the isolation airlock separating their lab from other parts of the complex.

Each knew from their training they had a maximum of thirty seconds to do this before the airlock door would be sealed. It had been drilled into them that if anyone missed the door sealing there could be no recovery until the lab had been fully cleared—in all likelihood leaving that person fatally exposed to contamination.

The year was 1980—a time when the Cold War between the Soviet Union and the West was at its height and many defense experts on both sides feared the onset of World War III.

In a part of the world remote from Moscow, but nevertheless vulnerable to invasion along its northern coastline, researchers were quietly investigating chemical and bio-agents in a top-secret installation hidden beneath the Garden Island Naval Base in the heart of Sydney, Australia. This was in spite of the universally accepted world convention prohibiting the use of bio-agents in warfare.

The laboratories were laid out at different levels in the complex with increasing protection measures against accidental infection. The biological agents were isolated from the working areas by purpose-designed bio-cabinets equipped with hand access ports, a system the risk analysts were confident provided 99.9% security for all those working in the lab, or anyone in the wider locality.

One winter morning their optimism was to be shattered.

« »

That same morning, Craig Wilkinson, a young biologist unaware of the critical situation at his workplace, was making his way to the installation from Circular Quay via the Botanic Gardens. He noticed a strange odor the moment he reached the middle of the Gardens. As he turned at a bend in the pathway, the strange smell was growing by the second, and a menacing cloud of black smoke was wafting his way. If he had been thinking more clearly he might have turned back and taken a different route to work, but as it was he was running late and decided to press on, pulling a handkerchief to his nose.

Passing the grove of tall Port Jackson fig trees close to the south-eastern entrance, a strange scene was unfolding. Men wearing protective gloves and face masks were sweeping up small furry objects and piling them into several forty-four gallon drums. They had obviously used kerosene as an accelerant and the putrid fumes made his eyes smart and his stomach heave.

As he got closer to one of the drums he could see that the men were incinerating dead fruit bats. Craig's curiosity was immediately piqued and, despite his nausea, he bent over one of the bats, noticing that its mouth was clamped shut in a death's grimace with red froth oozing from between its teeth. Unable to curb his overwhelming curiosity, he carefully touched the froth with the index finger of his left hand and sniffed, recoiling from the quite unfamiliar and powerful odor.

"I wouldn't touch that if I was you, mate!" yelled one of the workmen, his voice muffled by the face mask he was wearing.

"What happened to them?" he asked, curious to know whether the bats had been deliberately poisoned.

"Haven't a clue, mate. Something happened to them last night. We're burning the lot to reduce the risk of whatever it is from spreading to the other colonies."

« »

Within the administration wing of the installation an urgent meeting had been convened. The staff were of mixed ages, and the man who was chairing the meeting looked to be in his mid-fifties. His Australian accent was modulated by a slight twang, suggesting he had spent some career time in the United States. The atmosphere of the meeting was electric.

"I'm not pointing the finger," he said, despite the tone of his voice indicating otherwise, "but what I do require is an honest and objective assessment of the potential risks we are facing. Just how much HRNX-0 has escaped and how it happened—that's what I'd like to know."

"It seems that one of the maintenance team forgot to put back one of the filter panels in the exhaust system. Fortunately, the escape monitor triggered and the ventilation system was shut off immediately," said James, an intent and conservatively dressed young engineer. He punctuated his words with a flapping hand, making a turning motion like he was shutting off a valve.

"That's not all I asked, James," said the Chair. "Just how much got out?"

The young man's eyes involuntarily darted sideways as he tried to formulate a satisfactory answer. "We can't be sure, sir, but we estimate as much as ten grams may have escaped in the worst case scenario."

"In the *worst case scenario*," the Chair mimicked him angrily, "what impact is that likely to have on the thousands of people who are living and working near here?"

"I doubt that anyone's been able to make that assessment yet," said Craig, who had just joined the meeting from his encounter in the park, "but there is something that *is* potentially serious." His face was pallid and he was sipping from a glass of water with a visible tremor in his hand.

"Let us be the judge of that, Craig," said the Chair, quietly, in an authoritative tone.

"I usually walk through the Botanic Gardens on my way to work. This morning something was going on that didn't make sense. Some of the workmen were burning bats. There were piles of them. I checked one—not a pretty sight—looked like it had hemorrhaged and the blood had a very strange smell. I don't think those guys had any idea what it was and claimed they were burning them as a precaution against it spreading. If I'd known about this leak I would have been telling them to get the hell out of there, and I suppose…"

"Yep, we get the picture!" said the Chair without waiting for him to finish, and turned to the PA who was sitting next to him taking notes. "Cheryl, I want you to get in touch with the head of the Botanic Gardens, tell whoever it is that the men must stop burning the dead bats immediately, and get in here without delay. Stress that it's absolutely urgent and can't wait."

Craig's message and the Chair's reaction galvanized the meeting. No one knew where to look. Everyone was wondering whether they had somehow been responsible. One or two were jotting meaningless words on their scratchpads, unwilling to confront the worst possible scenario.

"We've got to nip this in the bud before news spreads, and put a clamp on anyone who has heard or seen what Craig has reported," the Chair continued. He turned back to his PA, who was looking hesitant. "What are you waiting for, Cheryl? Get on with it. Immediately!"

As she dashed out to do her boss's bidding, he closed the meeting, stressing, "I want everyone to stop what they've been doing and investigate all possible leads; doctors, hospitals, clinics, any place where someone who's been infected might have gone—leave no stone unturned. I cannot stress the absolute necessity: not a word of this gets out. It's a matter of utmost national security—your reports to me by this evening."

Craig had scrambled to his feet, clutching his stomach, and rushed towards the door. But he never made it, collapsing to the floor and doubling up in pain. Others jumped to assist, but by the time they had reached him he was already dead; eyes wide, and face contorted, his mouth frothing like the bats.

Absolute pandemonium erupted, some members of the meeting wringing their hands while staring helplessly at the body, others backing away in terror, but most realizing that their path to door was blocked were paralyzed in fright.

The fact that Craig was lying directly across the entrance was fortuitous. The Chair kept his head realizing that it would be catastrophic for a roomful of infected staff to make a run for anywhere outside the building. He picked up his communicator and called security ordering them to send someone to guard their entrance, notify their special medical emergency contacts and prevent anyone leaving the building.

The Chair was honest enough to realize his response was too little too late. He and his minions now contemplated the possibility of mass fatalities in the immediate vicinity of their research installation. But in one sense they were lucky. No information of what had occurred ever leaked into the public domain, and apart from Craig, there were no other recorded infections at that time.

PART 1

CHAPTER 1 Deployment: Nevada USA to Bourke NSW Australia

UFODD was not Byron Lowe's first career choice, and he wouldn't have contemplated it but for the fact he'd been fired by the online media company where he was previously employed. Without warning, when he showed up late for an important interview, his boss took him aside and said, "I'm letting you go Byron. You haven't turned out as I expected. You need a killer instinct for this job. I don't see it in you."

UFODD to give its full name was the *Unidentified Flying Object Defense Directorate*. Its main headquarters were located deep in the mountainous region of Nevada USA. Its mandate was simple—to identify any/all evidence of extra-terrestrial contact, suppress it at source and stem any potential leaks in the social or mainstream media.

Sam Mitchell was something of an outsider in the same class as Byron. With a PhD in Astrobiology from a University in Western Sydney, Australia, she had been headhunted and invited to enroll in UFODD's two year induction program, subsequently embarking on a new career of public disinformation.

The class that Sam found herself in was diverse in terms of gender and skills but mostly American and highly competitive. Sam got on well with most of her classmates with the exception of Byron, a slim-chested man with dark hair and a slight southern drawl.

Unlike Sam, Byron had a very privileged background. He had wealthy parents in Charleston, South Carolina, and until the economic downturn of 2028 had been free of the career challenges that faced most of his friends. Gifted with a great memory, he had breezed through his school and university years with limited effort.

After his dismissal from the publishing company he was working for, Byron returned to his family home in Charleston, taking up odd jobs to contribute to his extravagant social lifestyle. But the hatchet fell when his father caught him having breakfast late one morning.

"I'm not going to beat about the bush, son. I think it's time for you to make a new career for yourself. You may not realize it but my retirement fund has been hit in recent times, and I can no long afford picking up your tabs. Byron was thinking that his father must have made one too many bad investment decisions for his situation to have changed so suddenly, but resisted the urge to share his thoughts.

His father was feeling in his trouser pocket and finally pulled out his holo. You might like to take a look at this. It's the sort of challenge I think you need."

The holo was displaying an advert he'd saved. It read: 'UFODD is recruiting young Americans with curiosity, energy, and interests in global affairs. Our new recruits will attend an induction program, and on completion, take up global deployment opportunities…'

Byron quickly glanced at the advert and handed the holo back to his father. "That's not for me Dad, I'd sooner find something here."

Byron's father took a moment to respond. "Son, it's been difficult to cope since your mother died. And financial difficulties I can do without. From today I've closed your allowance, and I'm moving out of here into a smaller apartment. You will have to go somewhere else. Please take a closer look at that UFODD program.

His graduation from the UFODD induction program two years later was another wake-up call. As he sat down before Commandant Walter Berman, expecting a simple handshake and farewell, the man paused, staring at him with cold expression. "Cadet Lowe, your files tell me that at 31 you are one of the oldest in your class and have much more work experience than the others. We were expecting big things from you based on your first interview, however, having read your report and its critical comments, including some from fellow students, I have to say you could have done far better than you have. I'm angry because you've come across as the guy who takes it easy, always picking the shortest route between two points without looking around. And that's a very dangerous way to be in this line of business!"

He paused briefly to put his hand in the air to forestall any rejoinder from Byron.

"Cadet Lowe, you can take what I'm about to say as your first warning. If it were entirely up to me, I would probably have shown you the door, but you're in luck this time because someone whose opinions I respect persuaded me to give you another chance. So I've decided to deploy you about as far from the United States as possible. You'll be working within a region where you might actually be able to make a contribution, but if you don't it won't be the end of the world.

"At 0600 hours tomorrow you'll be joining your fellow cadet, Dr Samantha Mitchell, an Australian herself as you would know, and who will be able to show you around. You will be going to a remote town in New South Wales. It's called, Bourke, and close to where our HQ is located. There have been rumors of some new sightings around there but I doubt they will amount to anything.

"I'm appointing Samantha as the officer in charge. You will do exactly what she tells you. If there's a problem you'll be relieved of duties and there will be no further chances."

Berman rose to his feet and instead of offering to shake Byron's hand pointed towards the door. "Now get out of my sight!"

Byron marched out of the room with a hang-dog expression, for once in his life unable to think of how to react.

As Byron closed the door after him, Berman pondered whether he had made the right decision in choosing to partner Byron and Sam. The circumstance of their placement would require a lot of close proximity and cooperation. *Were they up to it?*

His misgivings were related to Sam's immediate reaction when he had given her the news during her own final interview.

"I have to say that Byron Lowe would have been my last choice to be partnered with. Throughout the induction program, he hasn't shown me or any of the other females any respect—in fact, to use one of our Australianisms, 'he's totally up himself'!"

Berman tried his best to paint a better picture. "Samantha, we've been hoping you might be able to turn him around once he's located away from his normal comfort zone and will have to rely on your obviously superior knowledge of local culture, geography and manners. And I can tell you confidentially that he's not stupid IQ-wise. He's one of the highest in the class in fact. We think that's a big part of his problem."

"I don't know what to say, Sir. I never imagined my job would include mollycoddling another student. I suppose I have no choice in this?"

Berman nodded his head.

"Well in that case, I want it recorded that I am going on this mission with very strong reservations. And if you'll pardon my French, if and when Byron fucks up, as I'm sure he will, it'll be on your head!"

« »

A waft of chilly air hit Sam and Byron as they emerged bleary eyed from the RAAF twin-electric shuttle to Bourke. By now it was close to midnight, local time. Their international flights had been complicated by news of a new pandemic disease discovered in Sydney requiring special permits to travel. They'd been held up in Singapore waiting for an RAAF plane to take them to Australia. Some 36 hours after they'd left USA they finally landed at The Richmond Air Base in Western Sydney, before their final leg to the small town in a remote corner of western New South Wales. As Sam explained to Byron en route, "Bourke was once a nerve center for the inland river trade. It's just an isolated backwater these days."

Briefly pausing at the head of the passenger stair, Byron was moved to remark on his first impressions including the intense blackness of a moonless night and the astonishing band of brilliant stars in the Milky Way.

Sam nodded, pausing to catch her breath. "Just smell that!" she exclaimed.

"Dust? Av-gas? Sweat?" he said, not getting what seemed so exciting.

"None of the above! Try again."

Byron was impatient to finalize their trip and had quite lost any sense of time, but to humor Sam he took a deep breath while shutting his eyes, as though he was sampling vintage wine. His expression became more animated. "What is that? Reminds me of some ointment we used when I was a kid?"

"It's the smell of eucalyptus trees, the oil in their leaves. Just catching a whiff of it now is such a turn on for me!"

"That's it!" he said. "Come to think of it we have our eucalypts all over the place back home…But I don't remember them smelling like this."

Sam was scanning across the tarmac to check out anyone there to meet them. She finally noticed a tall man walking towards them from what looked like the parking area to one side of the terminal. He was wearing a broad brimmed hat and walked with a slight limp. He was a man of few words, picked up two of their bags and escorted them to an ATV (All Terrain Vehicle) ready to make the final leg of their journey to UFODD's Base, "at the back of Bourke" as the man put it. Sam smiled, but the understated humor was lost on Byron.

"From what I've been hearing, you won't be getting much rest. The buzz is that there've been several new sightings," he remarked as they approached the outer fence to the compound surrounding the Base. It lay some 30km from Bourke, and was closely guarded by a tight-lipped detail of Hispanic Guards, who seemed to speak only Spanish.

The guards were using sign language and talked minimally amongst themselves as they escorted the pair to their barracks.

Sam nudged Byron indicating that she wanted to know what they were saying. He just ignored her.

"I thought you told me that you're fluent in Spanish?" Sam hissed.

"They've realized we're a special deployment and wondering what we're up to—that's all. But keep your voice down, it's best they don't know that I'm understanding them." said Byron conspiratorially.

« »

Despite their almost non-stop journey from the central United States and sense of disorientation, they were given little time to catch up on their sleep. They were woken at 0600 hours and given half an hour to report for duty.

They had no idea why the urgency, but could tell from the aide who came to get them that something was up.

He ushered them briskly into the meeting room without saying a word, where Commander Graves was waiting for them. He introduced himself as their new boss, a short man in his late fifties with thin greying hair and a penetrating stare through rimless glasses. He gave an immediate impression of taking no prisoners and had an impatient manner, quickly putting his new recruits on their guard.

"I'm glad you were able to join us," he said glancing at his watch. "Uneventful flight, I trust?" Without waiting for any answers, he proceeded to explain what was going on. "There've been more sightings, possible animal abductions. We've never seen anything quite like this before and…"

"What sort of sightings?" asked Sam.

"Curiously they're all linked to animals. The first two are peculiar incidents connected with dogs; the third is connected with bats. I want you to head for a small town called Wirrabera on the east coast, north of Sydney. You can start there. I want you to interview a man called Sens Petersen who seems to have been connected with the first incident. Here's the report."

Graves passed over a memory cube, to tap into their holos, then checked his watch. "It's 0700 now. Get going by 0800 and you will be at the RAAF Base nearest to Wirrabera mid-morning. I suggest you catch Petersen unawares and report to me tomorrow evening. We need to know whether or not he's implicated in that incident.

If he is, we'll decide what's best to do but I am thinking it will be a watching brief for now. Then you can proceed to South East Queensland where the other two sightings have taken place. Is that clear?"

"*Crystal*," remarked Byron.

Graves stared at him angrily.

"I'll put that impertinence down to jet-lag, son, but next time you can address me as 'Sir' – got that?"

"Yessir!"

"My secretary will confirm these orders and explain our comm. protocols. You may go now."

Once they were out of earshot of Grave's PA, Sam turned on Byron. "You realize that you've already pissed off the Camp Commandant with your attitude. I want to make something very clear, Byron. I'm the one in charge of these operations, not you, as clearly stated in our orders. From now on you'll leave all operational matters to me, otherwise you'll be on the next flight back to Base. Is that understood?"

"Yes Ma'am."

Sam knew he was still not respecting her but was reluctant to carry out her threat given the problems that would stir up. *Three strikes and he's out!* she thought to herself wearily.

CHAPTER 2 Pandemic and panic
Australia

Y*ou know you shouldn't bring that dog of yours in here don't you?*

Martha Smythe's voice was unbending but Sens knew that it concealed a soft heart despite her wanting to hide any signs of weakness.

"Marshall's on a lead as you can see. He's clean, and he promises not to make any trouble," Sens responded humbly.

"The moment I get a complaint you'll tie him up outside as you should have done in the first place. Do we understand each other?"

"Yes," said Sens in a quiet voice, "of course".

Sens endured this ritual every time he visited Wirrabera's 'Information Centre' as it was grandly titled. He knew better than to argue the toss and walked quickly past the checkout desk before Ms. Smythe changed her mind. He wandered to the back of the center where his favorite work station was unattended and made Marshall lie down where he would stay quietly at his feet for the hour or two it would take him to read all the news releases from Sydney London New York and wherever his interests would take him. He also needed to keep an eye on the state of the financial markets since he was in early retirement and depended on his investments. He could have done this from his own home a kilometer down from the town center to the beachfront where he also had good data access. But just like Marshall he needed to get out for exercise and interaction with others, even stroppy librarians.

The week before was the first time he'd learnt of a mysterious virus affecting staff and several guests in a large central Sydney hotel. Now what was being called a 'new pandemic' had spread quickly with a far higher percentage of fatalities than previous internationally transmitted pandemics such as the notorious COVID 19 virus more than a decade earlier. Sens was astonished to read how quickly the pandemic was spreading. The news item reported that any travelers without permits were being intercepted as they tried to leave Sydney. All state borders were similarly being policed.

Despite this, Sens had noticed that roads in and out of Wirrabera were unusually choked with cars. He had read local press reports of an increasing number of people arriving on the Maglev system, known as the 'MAG', and heard that all short stay accommodation in town was fully booked. Just ten days after the first outbreak was announced, the ATV as well as the Green Bus intercity bus network closed down, leaving the only option of walking, bike riding or the family vehicle.

Sens switched to some of the international feeds to discover that the new contagion was unprecedented for its exponential growth, simultaneously affecting every major city, from Singapore to Paris. Rapidly mounting numbers of people were succumbing to its deadly symptoms, most lasting for less than a few hours before going into coma and dying.

"You going to be much longer mate?"

Sens turned to see a young man with children in tow wanting to access the terminal. Marshall growled softly.

"Christ where did he come from!" The man's voice was unfriendly and he was definitely not a local judging by his posh accent. "Don't touch the dog Damian", he snarled at his ten your old boy who was bending down to pat him.

Sens put his hand on Marshall's collar to make sure he would not react. "You can have this terminal, I'm finished now," he said to the father, then turned to his son who was looking upset. "Marshall will not bite you, pat him if you like. But always be careful with strange dogs. Your Dad was right to warn you."

As Sens left the Centre and led Marshall back to their home, his thoughts returned to some of the reasons that had led to his choosing this part of the world and living a life that he would never have contemplated a few years before. His wife leaving him for someone else might have been avoidable but the second reason, a disease affecting his eyesight could not. It meant him having to give up a successful career as a pilot with QANTAS at a time when moving to a center far from the center of Sydney seemed more attractive than persisting with the urban rat race.

« »

One night, Sens had just finished eating and was moodily casting an eye over his scrupulously clean and tidy house. It had, perversely, begun to repel him to a degree. The company hiring bot-cleaners had been recommended by a friend of his at the local Men's Shed, lauding the benefits of having no more house tidying or cleaning to worry about. But maybe they were a little bit too efficient. His house seemed more like a medical clinic than a home.

Sens, for whom shopping was a chore, was fortunate in having sufficient food stocks to last him for two weeks, or a month if he went on a strictly rationed diet. He kept hoping that the pandemic would somehow go away, as the previous ones had, and was not taking it too seriously until he noticed the growing tide of people passing by his house or knocking on his door, begging for help. Sens was not an unkind man but resolutely decided against opening his door to strangers, fearing the outcome. On such occasions, having Marshall beside him was a big comfort.

As Sens and Marshall were finishing dinner in the kitchen at the rear of the house, someone started banging on the front door, shouting insistently, "give us some food, mate!" Sens remained quiet and did not move, although his heart was pounding. He had absolutely no intention of letting anyone in, and if they forced entry he could think of nowhere in the house that would make any sort of safe refuge. He glanced at Marshall whose ears were pricked up, listening acutely to the person's voice. Marshall eased himself to his feet and padded over to sit beside his master, growling softly at the intruders. Sens reached down to stroke his ears so that the growling did not become barking.

He could hear some chattering going on outside as if the person banging on his door had company; then he heard the distant wail of a police siren approaching. "Let's get out of here!" someone shouted, and the sound of running feet faded as the siren grew louder reaching an ear-splitting crescendo before it passed his house and was gone.

Sens' heart gradually stopped pounding, as he realized that the immediate crisis had passed. He fumbled in the fridge for a can of beer and went into the lounge to sit down in his favorite armchair with Marshall following him. He took a long swig of beer, relaxing slightly.

"What are we going to do, Marshall? If they had broken in we couldn't have stopped them taking everything, could we?" Marshall seemed to sense his master's anguish and laid his muzzle affectionately on his knee. Then without warning Sens' holo gave out an incoming message tone. He looked at the screen. It contained a message which read:

YOU ARE GOING TO HAVE TO DO SOMETHING ABOUT THIS, SENS.

Eerily, it was as if someone had been listening to his conversation with Marshall.

He spun his head expecting to see a face at the window or the sound of someone else at the door but there was nothing to explain where the message might have come from, or whether it was just somebody playing a practical joke. He felt a chill sense that he was being watched. *Who would be sending him so personal a message at this time, and who would it be who knew his contact details?* In consternation, looked again at the screen intending to re-read it, but it was gone. *Who could it be?*

Then when he turned to his dog Marshall, he noticed that he was staring back at him, intently, knowingly, with an expression he'd not seen before. It was as though the dog could understand exactly what was upsetting him.

A chaotic mixture of thoughts tumbled through Sens' head. His alarm at the intruder was replaced by a sense of the inexplicable. The possibility that Marshall was somehow involved in channeling messages to him via his holo was just too big a leap. Could it be that he was experiencing hallucinatory thoughts because he was now onto his third full-strength beer for the evening? He rose to his feet and backed out of the room on to the rear veranda, from which he could see above him a blazing dome of stars. It gave him a calming sense and a greater readiness to come to terms with what was going on.

Marshall had followed him out and was sitting on the veranda, his tail twitching slightly and his face wearing a slightly expectant look, as if he was waiting for a treat.

A new message appeared on Sens' holo:

YOU NEED NOT FEAR, THERE IS NOTHING WRONG WITH YOU OR MARSHALL. AS YOU HAVE RIGHTLY GUESSED, HE IS RELAYING OUR MESSAGES TO YOU.

Sens could only stare at Marshall in disbelief. He was unsure what to do. Should he say something aloud, or reply with his thoughts only?

This time he heard a response inside his head as though he was hearing the words in stereo sound.

There is no need for you to speak to us, if that makes you feel uncomfortable, the message continued. You need respond only with your thoughts. That will work just as well. And from now on, it will simplify matters if Marshall continues to transfer our thoughts to you directly rather than via your holo. That will be a far more secure way of communicating with you, now that you are beginning to understand more.

Who are you? What do you want? Are you a spirit or something? Sens thought, having watched various horror films about possession.

No, nothing like that. Actually, I am one voice representing what you might call a computer network or a nest of artificial intelligence nodes. You can simply call us a 'Nest' if you wish.

Sens was wondering how a computer network had somehow become connected with Marshall and himself. Who did it belong to? Was it about to threaten him? What did it want?

It was difficult to make any sense of what was taking place, or to believe that it was real. It was then that Sens made a crazy intuitive leap, remembering a film he had once watched long ago as a child, called '*Contact*'. A key scene in that film was when the heroine, played by Jodie Foster, had travelled to a distant part of the universe, where she was briefly reunited with a completely lifelike projection of the father she had lost as a child.

Sens recalled that her father was there to tell her about an alien civilization's purpose in making contact with the human race. In this humanized projection, it represented an intelligence that she was likely to believe and trust.

Are you extra-terrestrial? Sens ventured finally.

That is correct.

But why Marshall? Why invade my dog? Why didn't you take over a scientist, or politician, perhaps?

We have good reasons for doing it this way. Dogs aren't exactly threatening, and taking over a human would have greater consequences as I am sure you can understand.

Are there many of you? What do you want? Why have you chosen us to communicate with?

That's a lot of questions, Sens. I think you are going to understand the answers as we get to know each other better. If it helps, think of us as a singular identity rather than the collective intelligence that we really are.

For Sens this was an extremely unsatisfactory response. He had no idea why Marshall and he had been chosen as an intermediary between an extra-terrestrial AI Nest and the human population at large. All he knew was the only stopping him from reporting the matter to the authorities was the risk it might pose to Marshall.

CHAPTER 3 UFODD Special Agents visit Wirrabera

The twin-electric shuttle from Bourke to the closest airport to Wirrabera at Port Macquarie gave Sam and Byron a chance to read the brief police report provided to UFODD now stored on their holos. It was to the point.

Wirrabera Police Command

Incident Report

Date 30 March 2035

Summary

Alleged theft of 4 pedigree puppies by Sens Petersen, Wirrabera resident.

Date of the alleged incident: 23 March 2035.

Conclusion

Allegation of Sens Petersen's complicity in theft remains unproven, although some circumstantial evidence is corroborated.

Details

Pat Willingham, owner of **PetsLikeUs** Wirrabera alleged Petersen was responsible for a clever prank/theft of 4 pedigree sheep dog pups from his store last Saturday morning.

Willingham stated the man and his kelpie visited his store and were particularly interested in his latest litter of kelpie puppies. He thought the man was muttering something to his dog as all the pups in the display area were crowding together wanting to be let out and play. Willingham mentioned that the pups were valuable pedigrees worth 'thousands of dollars apiece'.

As the man and his dog were in his shop, a blackout occurred which Willingham thought was caused by the 30+ degree conditions experienced that day. He also mentioned it had gone very dark outside, 'as if an eclipse was happening.'

Note: the following description by Willingham has been corroborated in the attached clipping from Wirrabera Times.

Willingham said that, when he looked through the shop window, he could see people running around as though they were scared about something. Some other observers reported seeing the dark silhouette of a cigar shaped craft in the sky. It hovered for a short period above them, before vanishing from sight.

Willingham states that his attention was distracted for several moments, but when he turned to see whether the man and his dog wanted to buy one of his pups, he had already left the store, and there was no sign of his pups in the enclosure.

Wirrabera detectives have since examined the enclosure and confirm that it is constructed of 15 mm Plexiglas, incorporating a locked entry gate. Willingham is the only one in possession of the combination. There was no sign of breakage or forced entry into the enclosure, or any damage to the shop window, which backs onto the enclosure.

Willingham further states he assumed that the man and his dog were somehow connected with the robbery of his pups although he had no direct evidence of that. He ran outside and observed him and his dog walking some distance away, towards the Wirrabera Foreshore. He pursued him and accused him of stealing his pups. But the man denied any wrongdoing.

We have since conducted our own interview of the accused, Sens Petersen. Petersen has no criminal record and has been a resident of Wirrabera for some years with no previous concerns or attentions from Wirrabera Police Command. In his former career he was a respected pilot employed by QANTAS, retired for health reasons.

Petersen claims to have been unaware that puppies had disappeared and had no involvement in their disappearance. He offers no explanation of the incident. He does confirm having visited the shop and his own dog showing interest in the puppies. But as he points out, that would have been an entirely natural and expected aspect of dog interaction and behaviour.

Other witnesses (one of whom had noticed Sens and his dog) were unable to corroborate Willingham's claim that the man had any pups in his possession or concealed on his person.

Rodney Jensen

Recommendation

It is recommended that there be no finding of wrongdoing by the accused and no satisfactory explanation of the events reported by various sources. This report should remain confidential pending fresh evidence or further inquiries.

Sam absent-mindedly picked at a tooth, staring into space, deep in thought. Then she turned to Byron who had just put down his holo. He stared back at her with a look of bemusement.

"What do you think, Byron?"

"Several strange aspects; for a start, is the shopkeeper deluding himself about the amount he's claiming for these pups? Could this simply be an insurance fraud?

"Then there's this Sens character. Can he be as innocent as he claims? I get the feeling that he knows far more than he's letting on. It seems more than a coincidence that his dog should have been interacting with those puppies just before they disappear. And then there's the UFO sighting which several observers have already corroborated not just in this police report but by our liaison staff with Australian Commonwealth Investigations. Then of course there's the blackout. My take is that there's a connection there, that can't be coincidental. We've just got to work out what it is, and Petersen has to be the starting point."

"Yes there was another file from the Australian Weather Centre which states no eclipse was projected for the time when the skies were reported to have gone dark. I'm coming to a similar conclusion about this man. He's hiding something for sure. And it can't be a coincidence that there's this ET occurrence was timed at the same time the pups disappeared."

"I agree, let's surprise him," said Byron.

Sam had by now turned her attention to one of the news services on her holo. "Hey check this out!" she showed Byron the headline which read:

'POLICE CORDON SURROUNDS SYDNEY'

The report stated that any traveler without an official permit was being turned back at all roads leading out of the metro area. All state borders were similarly being policed.

"I've been following news from the States as well. The reports are saying that it's jumped there starting in LA. We're lucky to be based in the outback.

"Actually much closer to home, I'm really worried about my mother," said Sam.

"You've not mentioned her before?"

"She lives by herself in the Blue Mountains and I haven't seen her for three years. I avoided telling her I'd be coming home and there's been no chance of my making a visit. But maybe this current situation might give me more leverage with Graves."

"This Wirrabera place could also be vulnerable to anyone who's trying to get out of Sydney." Byron remarked. "I'd wait until we've reported on the situation there before trying any personal requests on Graves. I don't see him as the sentimental type."

"Byron for once we're in agreement! But I'm going to have to try approaching him when the time's right."

"Just watch out for the toilet paper and convenience food in the Centers—they'll be the first to go!"

"I'm just hoping that we won't be here long enough for that to be a concern. Just make sure you have a face mask in your pocket and wear it at this next interview."

"Yes Mom," said Byron.

« »

The man who came to the door was above average height and wore a neatly clipped beard. He was wearing a large straw hat and overalls looking like he might be Petersen's gardener rather than the man they were after.

"If you've come about a market survey or want to convert me to your religion, I'm not interested," he said as he half opened the door and caught sight of Sam and Byron wearing somber civilian clothes.

"Mr. Sens Petersen?" Sam asked him. Sens nodded, with a wary expression.

"We're following up a recent inquiry into some missing animals. Your name came up in Wirrabera Police Command's report into the incident. May we come inside and discuss this?"

Sens made no move to let them in from his position behind the door, his expression far from welcoming. "Who are you? What organization do you work for?"

Sam produced her warrant card and showed it to him. "We are agents for UFODD, an international agency that investigates unexplained sightings and events. Can we have a few words with you?" she asked.

"I have already been interviewed by the police about the incident. I suggest that you go and talk to them. I have nothing more to tell you," he said.

Byron put his hand up to prevent Sens from shutting the door in their faces.

"We have read the police report, but we need to go over some of the points with you. We can see that you are reluctant to discuss this with us, but if you continue to obstruct our inquiries we will have no alternative but to require you to accompany us to our offices, where we will interview you more formally." Sam said.

Sens allowed them to follow him through into his lounge. It was sparsely furnished with two armchairs, a dining table and a bookcase with several framed images of international landmarks in Singapore, Paris and London. They heard soft growling noises from the corner of the room where a black sheep dog with white paws was standing next to a basket, his ears pricked up, watching them intently.

"You sure he isn't going to take a chunk out of us?" asked Byron. "He seems to be taking a remarkable interest in us."

Rodney Jensen

"Don't mind Marshall. He's very well trained, and friendly once he gets to know you. Just ignore him," said Sens, and invited the two to sit down at the dining table.

« »

Sam led the interview with Byron sitting to her right. She had her recorder and a scratch pad to jot down anything she noticed in Sens' reactions.

"We'd like to hear your account of what happened when you visited the pet store where you've been accused of stealing puppies."

Sens reacted angrily. "When the police interviewed me before, I explained everything. What else do you need to know now?" he began.

"Look at it from our point of view," said Sam. "A man and his dog go into a pet shop and show a keen interest in some puppies on display. The shop owner is distracted for a short time by something very strange occurring outside including skies going dark in the middle of the day and a UFO appearing and disappearing. The owner goes back into the shop and his pups have disappeared. You have also left the shop while the man was distracted. You're an intelligent man, I'm sure. Do you seriously expect us to believe that these events are not connected? Now can we start again and hear your version of what actually that took place."

Sens took several moments to consider how to respond. "I can see what you are thinking, and I am as much in the dark as you are. I have no idea what was going on and have no explanation of where those pups went or who took them."

"The shop owner mentioned he saw you muttering something to your dog – Marshall, isn't it, while he was attracting the attention of the pups in their enclosure."

"Seriously? What's unusual about that? I talk to Marshall all the time. He's an intelligent dog, my best friend. We talk a lot, and he understands me perfectly. He just wanted to take a good look at the puppies. It's normal for dogs to do that. Have you ever owned a dog yourself? Doesn't seem like you have, otherwise you wouldn't be asking me such ridiculous questions!"

Byron's face had turned pink and he seemed about to make some unpleasant remark about Sens' mental capacity, but Sam put her hand up to shut him up.

"And you're quite sure that you're not holding something back from us? Particularly about your dog and the strange events which occurred outside the shop at exactly the same time you were present and the puppies disappeared?" Sam asked.

Sens just shook his head angrily.

"I never planned what took place. I was in the main street browsing windows. 'PetsLikeUs' is Wirrabera's only pet shop, and was open despite many other shops closed because of the looters. I'd been there before because they had a secret recipe for dog biscuits which they sell by the sack-full. When we went into the shop the manager asked me to keep Marshall on his lead because he was already exciting his puppies. They were kept in a glass enclosure next to the shop window. I noticed about four pups and a sign on the enclosure was offering to sell two for the price of one."

"Did you go close to the enclosure, close enough to work out that there were four of them?" Sam persisted.

"No I was standing at the counter all the time with Marshall sitting next to me. "I was about to order my bag of dog biscuits when I happened to notice something strange happening in the street. There were several people pointing up at the sky and looking excited. My curiosity got the better of me and I excused myself explaining to the man at the counter that I wanted to see what was going on."

"And that was the last you saw of the puppies?" Meg asked.

"Yes it was. Marshall and I went outside and it soon became obvious why everyone was so excited."

"The UFO?" Byron asked.

"Not immediately. The first thing like a solar eclipse was taking place. It was difficult to see around the street because the sky had suddenly gone very dark. It was dark enough to make the sun difficult to see, but then I did see the faint outline of a cigar-shaped craft."

"If you could hardly see the sun, how were you able to see this craft?" asked Sam.

"It had a faint luminosity too. But suddenly, there was a searchlight coming from it, and we all had to look away. It was only on for less than a minute but switched off suddenly leaving us dazzled for quite a while. Then it was no longer dark as though it were mid-day again. When I looked up at the sky where the craft had been. It was gone"

"Then what happened?" Sam asked.

"The man who'd been serving me at 'PetsLikeUs' came running out and accused me of stealing his pups. I had no idea what he was talking about at first. Then he started shouting and pointing at me like I was a thief. He claimed they had all gone when I left the shop and was certain I was responsible."

"I denied this and Marshall and I walked off while he was still ranting away that he would 'get even' or something like that. I had a call from the police later that day. They searched this house and couldn't find anything. And now you're here. You seem to be intelligent people and apart from the disappearance of those pups I'm pretty sure you would have corroborated the other things I've told you. How do you suppose I could possibly have removed those puppies, all four of them, given what actually happened once I left the store?" Sens had been playing with Marshall's lead absentmindedly, and had kept sipping from a glass of water during the meeting. He seemed distracted and ill at ease.

"That's exactly why we are talking to you," said Sam. "Do you have any explanations?"

"Of course I have thought about it. The first, perhaps most obvious one, is that the store manager was lying but I don't really believe that. He seemed genuinely convinced that I was to blame enough to make a detail report of the episode to the police. I don't think he would have done that if he'd been involved."

"Nor do we," said Byron, and Sam nodded.

"That leaves what most people would think is an even wilder possibility, that the UFO's appearance is the connection. Somehow it was able to abduct the pups," said Sens.

Sam and Byron looked at each other. Finally Sam broke the silence. "All I can say is that we're checking all avenues of inquiry. The appearance of that UFO is certainly a mystery. Your suggestion that it's behind the pups disappearance is without any evidence."

She and Byron got to their feet, as though they were about to leave. Then Sam paused and turned to Sens. "I'm still having difficulties with what you've told us Mr. Petersen and. I'm unconvinced by your explanation. You need to be aware that there are severe penalties for hindering our inquiries into this matter. I have a strong feeling that you're hiding something. Just be aware that we'll not rest until we get to the bottom of it. Would you show me your holo, please?"

Sens dug it out of his pocket and held it out to her. Sam tapped her own against his and handed his holo back to him.

"There! You now have my contact details, and I invite you to use them, once you've had time to consider what I've just told you. Hopefully you will do this before we take the matter further."

She gestured to Byron and they left.

Sens sat brooding at his table, with the weight of the world on his shoulders. Suddenly it seemed to him that the Nest was not exactly the benign invader it had portrayed. It was becoming increasingly obvious that there was an agenda that was not being explained. He could not imagine why they had abducted the puppies from the pet shop, or why they had chosen Marshall as their intermediary. When Sens tried to get an explanation, there was a wall of silence that had even more worrying implications than if the Nest had merely tried to brush the matter off. Sens remembered how the Japanese in past decades had manipulated the media by justifying their ongoing whale slaughter as the basis of 'scientific research'. Did the Nest have similar intentions?

CHAPTER 4 Departure from Wirrabera

Sens' relationship with Marshall had changed. The elusive happiness and contentment he had shared with his dog seemed lost forever. He felt naked and exposed now that an alien presence was reading his innermost secrets, morning till night. He was on 'just nodding' terms with his next-door neighbor, he had no close friends to confide in and dreaded what might become of Marshall if he did tell anyone.

Equally disturbing was the mounting impact of the pandemic on Wirrabera and its surrounds. All around him were signs of desperation and threat from homeless people seeking refuge from Sydney. His life in Wirrabera, which had always been quiet and peaceful, now seemed to be on the fringe of a catastrophe. He felt a sense of frustration and resentment but could think of no easy fix short of heading off and leaving it all behind, which he did not want to do.

Faced with a situation which he neither understood nor knew how to address, he began to retreat and do nothing. The bot-cleaner services had disappeared along with many other minor industries that the pandemic had impacted. His house quickly became a disorganized mess. He stopped eating regular meals, forgot to wash himself regularly, or wear anything but his dressing gown and slippers. He would sit around all day, staring moodily into space, hoping that the pandemic would go away. Most of all, he wanted to be rid of the Nest and have Marshall to himself.

One evening, after Sens had spent virtually the whole day in this semi-catatonic state, staring moodily into space and doing nothing but sitting around, Marshall sat down beside him with an anticipatory look in his eyes.

Sens, listen to me. The voice of the Nest cut across his reverie, making him both annoyed and fearful at the same time.

Leave me alone. You are not welcome here. Go and bother someone else, he thought moodily.

Marshall can sense that there is something very wrong with you. And I can also see that your sensory system is ignoring your normal stimuli—it is as though you are asleep, but you are awake. What is the matter?

What's it to you? Sens responded.

You are facing a situation you cannot ignore, said the Nest. *It will not solve itself. If you do not act, you will die of starvation before long, or someone who is stronger and more determined than you will break in and steal all your remaining food. What will you do then? You have no plans, have you?*

I suppose I don't, admitted Sens flatly, *other than go somewhere else where there are fewer people to deal with. But why should I move? I used to love it here.*

I think that your idea of moving away does have merit, said the Nest, ignoring the anguish that had crept into Sens' thoughts. *I have detected traces of memory of a relative who lives a long way from here who you might stay with?*

Sens thought for a few moments, wondering who the Nest could possibly be referring to. *Raegan! Is that who you mean? He's the only person I can think of—lives somewhere out west. I haven't seen him since we were kids.*

That corresponds with the memory—yes, said the Nest. *I think it would be an ideal place to wait out this situation, don't you?*

Sens' immediate reactions were a mixture of—*Not a great idea, there are heaps of problems in the current pandemic in making such a trip. And what about my house? If I leave it like this someone will break in and steal everything. And if I do go my old ATV might not make it. It's on its last legs and hasn't been serviced for the past five years!*

The Nest simply brushed all these negative thoughts aside with: *We must address such challenges if and when they arise, but at least you should make a start. You cannot stay here. Of that we are certain.*

Sens chose to ignore the Nest's advice and planned to stay in Wirrabera. But it was not long after this conversation that circumstances forced him to change his mind. He had woken one morning feeling slightly less depressed and decided to take Marshall out in the aluminum dinghy, or 'tinny' as it was called. It was a huge relief for Sens to get out of the house and leave the problems of the world temporarily behind. They had caught a few fish, which were a welcome addition to their dwindling food stores. The only marring aspect of the day had been the need for constant bailing of seawater seeping through the corroded hull.

By mid-afternoon he finally decided to call it a day. His elbow and shoulder were aching from the bailing, making it very difficult for him to fire up the small outboard motor and heave the tinny back onto the rack beside the beach once they had come ashore.

As he headed along the street where his house was located, he saw it was on fire. Black clouds of smoke could be seen billowing out of smashed windows. Water was cascading down the walls, carrying streaks of ash and grit after it and draining into a gushing stream of water running down the gutter. A robo-fire truck was ineffectively landing a spray of water over the main seat of the fire. One or two men in yellow protective jackets and helmets were holding people back from the site, no doubt including a growing crowd of opportunists hoping to salvage something useful from the blaze.

Sens broke into a run, but his way was blocked by a large and immovable fireman. "It's not safe, mate!" he shouted. "You'll have to wait until we've got it under control."

Sens could only stand by helplessly, as he watched the roof collapse and his house turn to a heap of smoldering rubble before his eyes. All the treasured possessions he had stored in the attic going with it.

Sens started to shout something at Marshall in his distraught state, forgetting that people were watching him. "Were you behind this?" he raged. "This can't be a coincidence, can it?"

Of course not, the Nest replied. *You will discover that the dishwasher you left on before you went out has an electrical defect— it was a badly corroded power plug which started the blaze. They cause far more fires than most people realize. Anyway, I suggest that you calm down and give Marshall a pat—you wouldn't want to land in a mental hospital, would you?*

Rodney Jensen

People were indeed staring at Sens, wondering if the stress had made him delusional. The fireman who had prevented him from racing into his house took him by the arm and said in a kindly voice: "We'll have it under control soon, mate. Have you anywhere you can go?"

Sens stared at the man unseeingly—he had no relatives nearby and no particular friends. He caught himself in a wave of disbelief, swaying and feeling unsteady with the shock.

« »

With no house, nowhere else to stay and his only food being some bulk stores he had left in the garage, the idea of moving far away suddenly seemed the best and only option. Sens decided to leave immediately, hoping that he would be well to the west of Wirrabera by late evening.

He raided his garage for anything that might be useful on his journey. Then, turning his back on the shell of his burnt out home, he opened the door of his ATV for Marshall to jump in, and set off with a mixture of emotions and a sense that he would never be coming back.

As they headed west in the direction of the setting sun, Sens had plenty of time to ponder what might have really caused the fire, and whether or not to believe the Nest's explanation. From his work in the aircraft industry he knew a lot about electrical circuits, making him suspicious of the defective plug explanation. If that had been correct, he was sure that he would have noticed it overheating before. His experience told him that he would recognize a seriously overheated plug or appliance by the distinctive, unpleasant smell they made.

But there had been nothing like that. If the defective plug was not really the reason for the fire, his suspicions again fell on the Nest, particularly given that they were such a strong advocate for him leaving. In some obscure way, leaving Wirrabera, and heading off to Bourke, seemed to form part of the Nest's plan for him and Marshall, although for the life of him, he couldn't see why.

CHAPTER 5 An unexpected turn

The route Sens chose from the coastal town of Wirrabera near Port Macquarie to the bush town of Bourke in the heart of rural New South Wales, followed a westerly track via back roads to Tamworth, and on through Narrabri, Walgett, and Brewarrina.

In normal times it would have been possible to travel this route in a single day, but the conditions were far from normal in these pandemic times. The journey ended up taking far longer, mainly because the usual facilities for battery recharge had been suspended. It was fortunate that the Bravura Honda Sens owned had integrated solar panels which greatly extended the range of the on-board battery system.

They passed very few other vehicles once they left the Pacific Highway, although there were occasional groups of cyclists carrying backpacks and some people on foot. Many of these were hitch hiking, carrying signs indicating where they wanted to get to, and waving hopefully at Sens as he passed them. But his ATV was crammed with camping gear and other belongings, and he could not bring himself to slow down or stop to help. "It's too big a risk," he said to Marshall, feeling guilty that he could be accused of callous disregard for others in even worse need than him.

After leaving the coast they climbed laboriously up the slopes and across the Great Dividing Range before reaching plateau country surrounding Tamworth. Sens decided to skirt around Tamworth, ending up halfway between the small settlements of Bendemeer and Manilla. By this time it was well after dark and the warning light on the dashboard was shining bright red, registering that they had less than ten kilometers worth of driving left in the power system.

Sens found a narrow track and drove along it a few hundred meters so as to be out of sight. He let Marshall have a run around while he collected some firewood and put up a tent for the night. They felt the cutting embrace of a cold westerly and huddled almost on top of the feeble flames of the campfire. A scratch meal of dog biscuits and water for Marshall, a burnt chop and sausage for Sens, left nothing much to do but retire to the shelter of the tent. Sens scrambled awkwardly into his musty sleeping bag and Marshall lay down beside him, with a blanket thrown over. Marshall was soon snoring loudly, making it hard for Sens to relax and sink into sleep.

With the first part of the journey over, it was hard to dispel the vision of endless road and the pathetic signs of people fleeing from Sydney along it. He was also forced to face what he had previously put aside, and could no longer ignore—the fact that he had become effectively homeless and left with nothing but the few belongings he could cram into his medium-sized ATV. There was also a looming threat that his interviewers from UFODD were on his trail. He would stick to the back roads at least until he had found a new bolt hole to hide in.

In the middle of the night Sens was woken by a particularly loud whimper from Marshall clearly in the midst of a nightmare. Even after his dog's breathing had returned to its normal rhythm, the disturbance left Sens awake, with busy thoughts of whether the world might ever return to normality, or what on earth could the Nest have in store for him and Marshall.

Rodney Jensen

« »

The next day Sens and Marshall set off again on the next leg of the journey to Bourke. The salt pans and flat irrigation areas surrounding the Namoi River and Narrabri gradually gave way to scrubby plains, then to even sparser spinifex.

Putting aside the looming presence of the Nest, Sens was feeling more liberated and relaxed about moving on. His mood was also lifted by what he was seeing along the way, particularly the sense of space created by the flat plains and the endless straight road ahead receding to a tiny point in the shimmering distance. The bare ochre colored earth reminded him of numerous Australian and indigenous artists whose paintings embraced earth colors as their trademark of Australian Country.

They stopped briefly at an abandoned railway station somewhere between Narrabri and Walgett. Sens felt a sense of sadness that the remnants of an ambitious railway network had long since been made redundant with advances in transport technology. He reflected that long before he was born, the daily arrival of a train would have been met by a bevy of people and goods brought in from the surrounding countryside by horse and cart.

All that was left were derelict buildings surrounding the rusted rails lying on rotted or missing timber sleepers. The squared stone walls of the railway office had survived, but had become almost submerged under luxuriant weeds and scrub. With its blind windows and the station platform bare of waiting passengers, the place struck a surreal note in such a lonely, otherwise featureless, semi-desert country.

Marshall bounded around, delighted to escape his close confines. Sens stretched his weary muscles and aching joints, unused to the pressure of driving such long distances hour after hour.

"Come on, Marshall," shouted Sens when he could see that true to his disgusting dog nature, he had discovered a juicy sheep pat to roll in. Marshall ignored him and began furiously scratching himself. Sens fumbled in the boot of his ATV to bring out a bowl and fill it with water from his plastic jerry can. As he bent down to put the bowl on the ground, Marshall bounded over, anxious to slake his thirst and lap up the water, splashing drops in all directions. As Sens was leaning down, he felt a sudden pinprick on his skin, like an ant was on his neck. He slapped it away absently and thought nothing more of it as the pain receded.

The drive continued along a highway as straight as an arrow, with abundant wildlife grazing on the few remnant grass shoots on both sides of the road. Big grey kangaroos and smaller wallabies stood up on their hind legs staring at them as they drove past, and Sens, a careful driver at the best of times, slowed right down, knowing how common it was for them to jump right in front of oncoming vehicles at the last moment. Many carcasses on the roadside were proof of this suicidal behavior. There were emus in the distance as well as flocks of wild goats and sheep in some places, but these seemed to react more sensibly by turning to flee from the oncoming ATV in the opposite direction.

As they were travelling the last few kilometers into Bourke, the distant profile of Mount Oxley appeared on the left-hand side of the road, its peak glinting redly in the light of the setting sun. Sens turned his head to look more closely at it, but as he straightened up to look back at the road ahead he felt a slight wash of dizziness and for a moment, the ATV veered onto the shoulder before he realized what was happening. He slowed down, stopped by the side of the road and turned off the motor.

What is wrong with you? The soft voice of the Nest seemed dreamlike to Sens.

I don't know, I need to stop, he said as the dizziness returned.

The world receded into blackness…

« »

Sam and Byron were back in Wirrabera two days after Sens had left. Sam had tried to call his holo twice to follow up their interview and finally called the local police.

DCI Barnes took the call. "I should have let you know before but there has been a development. Your contact Sens Petersen's house burnt down in what can only be described as suspicious circumstances. Petersen has no relatives or particular friends who he could have stayed with we've discovered. Even his next door neighbors had little contact with him. Maybe he was in a state of shock when he found his place burnt to the ground, but he appears to have packed up most of his stuff in his ATV and done a bunk. Nobody knows where he's gone, but I have a strong feeling that he won't be back soon."

Now the two were staring at ruins of Sens burnt out home. "Whatever caused that fire did a thorough job,"

Byron remarked. The modest two bedroom weatherboard cottage they had visited recently was now a pile of charcoal, smashed glass and twisted roof metal. A garage to the rear showed scorch marks on the side facing where the house had been but was otherwise intact. Sam tried the door and it swung open.

"This looks like it's been cleaned out too." Sam said. She kneeled on the concrete floor to look more closely, and pointed out some oil marks in one place.

"Probably the sump had a leak," said Byron.

"The thing that surprises me is that there is almost nothing left in this garage. It looks completely cleaned out and if our man had a standard sized vehicle I don't think he could have fitted the sort of things most people accumulate into it?" Sam continued. "My guess is that he would have kept at least some food stores in here, possibly camping gear, which he might have been able to find space for, but what about lawnmowers, tools, bicycles and barbeques. There can't have been enough space for those sort of things. The police mentioned this to me and have also checked with the neighbors. They think he either took the bulky stuff to the tip or more likely some of those roaming refugees have helped themselves."

CHAPTER 6 More UFO sightings

Special Agents Lowe and Mitchell were given little time after their return from Wirrabera to prepare themselves for their journey to Southeast Queensland, where the various UFO sightings had been reported. By the time they had fastened their seatbelts in the latest model TEC (twin electric copter) they were completely exhausted and almost past caring what lay ahead. Fortunately, their pilot wasn't talkative.

It took them almost half the journey before they could take in what was going past them some 1000 meters below, at the craft's cruising speed of 350 km/hr. The track between UFODD Base and their destination was mostly over semi-desert country. From the air it looked like a burnt ochre sandscape, endlessly stretching in all directions. The only distinctive features were the occasional ruler-straight stretches of tarmac road, and a spider's network of watercourses. Sam was able to share with Byron her understanding that this was ancient terrain, and after years of prolonged drought it might as well have been the surface of Mars.

From time to time, they passed tiny settlements located at some significant crossing point or other, mostly a watercourse. For Sam, some of the place names they were reading off their holos brought back history of the early explorers she'd learnt at school. Both the towns of St George and Miles had a distinctive layout as seen from the air, with a large grid of local roads close to the inland river system. Even from the air these towns had a timeless look about them, with not an apartment building in sight. The houses, looking more like homesteads, lay surrounded by very large gardens, and the streets that they were fronting seemed wide enough to accommodate twenty Clydesdale horses with a bullock wagon in tow.

One hour further into the journey, the searing heat of this semi-desert country gave way to an expanse of grey-green bushland, and the TEC began its descent. It came gently to earth in a clearing in the forest located at the peak of a low mountain. They could see a steel lattice structure surmounted by an observation deck high above them. A man was waiting for them at the foot of the tower.

He was very tall and dressed in a regulation military style khaki shirt and slacks held up by a broad leather belt equipped with a knife holster. His eyes and face were hidden behind very dark Polaroid glasses and a black face mask. He was wearing a navy blue peaked baseball cap bearing the gold-embroidered words: 'Park Ranger'. He could have looked quite smart but somehow his clothes had a 'slept in' look and it was obvious that he didn't care. Byron looked him up and down with a poorly disguised air of superiority.

"Welcome to Barakula State Forest, I'm Ted Bridges, and here to look after you," he said.

Byron shrugged while Sam introduced them, and they followed him into a slow lift that carried them to an observation pod perched atop the tower.

"Wow!" said Byron, his attitude changing. "Big, huh!" He was staring out at the immense forest wilderness that stretched to the horizon as viewed in a 360 degree panorama from the observation windows. The windows were of tinted glass and angled like those in an old-style aircraft control tower. Byron walked around the perimeter of the pod, staring in all directions with childish enthusiasm. Sam was playing it cool, and took up a position looking away from the rising sun, which was making her already bloodshot eyes feel ever more like they'd been rubbed over with sandpaper.

"It's the largest state forest in the southern hemisphere—260,000 hectares in total," Bridges said. He clearly felt ill at ease, for reasons that were not immediately apparent, and played with his cap, waiting to see what his guests wanted. "You might care to use these," he said, handing each of them a pair of state-of-art electronic, optically stabilized, ultra high zoom binoculars with night vision capability.

"Wow," Byron repeated, "totally awesome!" He began looking through the binoculars and zooming in on distant features, completely absorbed.

"Now getting back to business," said Sam, pointedly glaring at Byron. "So was it you who reported the sighting?" she asked, still impatient with her partner's immature behavior.

"Yes, I sent in the report. My shift normally runs from midnight 'til eight. Geoff was delayed because his wife's having a baby, but messaged in to say he'd get here when he could."

"And Geoff is?" Sam asked.

"We run eight-hour shifts and Geoff replaces me each morning, except on this occasion, and Kevin comes on at four."

"Do you always work by yourselves?"

"Nearly always. The only time we have company is when there's something like a bushfire. Then it gets busy and we'll need at least two pairs of hands (or more) to coordinate what's going on."

"Can you tell us what it was you saw, and when?" asked Byron, finally putting down his binoculars with some reluctance.

"It was about two in the morning." Ted hunted for a piece of scribbled paper sitting on the central communications console. "02:07 it was when I first saw an intense light bearing seventy-four degrees and heading this way."

"The light?" said Byron impatiently.

"A cone of light coming from somewhere. Even with the glasses on it, it was difficult to be certain where it was coming from. The source of the light was just too intense to look at, particularly through the glasses."

"Could it have been army or air force manoeuvres?" asked Sam, already knowing the answer from the file she had scanned on the journey.

"Definitely not. They would need a special permit for operations of any sort in State Forest, and there's never been anything like that on my watch. In any case, they have their own extensive areas they use for exercises in the bush," said Ted.

"I suppose at this distance it would have been difficult to see, but could you see the shape of a craft of any sort?

I know you said that the brightness of the light made it difficult to see, but could you make out anything above the cone of light?"

Sam was thinking about the report of the craft that had been observed in the sky above the pet shop in Wirrabera.

"No as I said that light blotted everything out around it."

"What do you think it was then?" pressed Sam.

"I've no idea. I've never seen anything like it before in my life. Strangely, the beam of light lasted for about thirty seconds only. Then it switched off, whatever it was."

"I don't suppose you'd be in a position to accurately locate where this light hit the ground?" asked Byron, as though he were expecting a 'no'.

"Yes," said Ted. "I've plotted the bearing and range for you here. 'X marks the spot', as they say."

He handed them a large-scale aerial photograph showing the position relative to the tower. "As you can see, there's an access track about three kilometers from that spot, but we can bush-bash the final bit if you want?"

The two nodded in agreement.

« »

The journey to their target was made easier than it might have been, courtesy of Ted's all-terrain ground effect vehicle. It was ideally suited to the narrow, rocky fire trail that took them to the closest point they could get to by road. At one point Ted had to stop when the road ahead was blocked by a fallen tree. But it was the work of only a few minutes for him to chainsaw the trunk and tow it out of the way with the tow rope he carried for just this purpose.

The forest was not a part of Australia Sam was familiar with, and for Byron, it was a journey of discovery in which everything was new and fascinating. The aromatic smell of the dense blackbutt and spotted gums, the occasional song of an unknown bird and the relentless rasping chant of huge noisy cicadas heightened the sense of isolation and wilderness. Ted had been studying his GPS and finally pulled to a stop. With the sound of the engine gone, there was a sudden stillness, disturbed only by the rasping cicadas. The encircling high trees prevented any direct sunlight reaching them.

"I wouldn't want to be alone here on a dark night," muttered Byron softly.

"You thinking about the axe murderer?" said Sam. But her in-house humor was lost on him.

"Axe murderer?" he said blankly.

"There have been quite a few cases where I came from in NSW, state forests just like this—people going missing, usually tourists. Some finally tracked down and recovered—hacked to bits. Those responsible were eventually banged up and never released. Places like this seem to attract nutters for some reason," she said.

Rodney Jensen

"It must be the isolation," commented Byron, "brings out the primeval state—man against man with only clubs or spears to defend themselves. Constant threats from tigers or mammoths you know! Come to think of it," he continued, "I remember a few cases near where I come from—people disappearing—parts of their bodies floating to the surface after years of being weighted down in a swamp—stuff like that." Byron seemed to be enjoying himself but Sam was regretting she had ever mentioned the axe murderer.

Her dark thoughts were interrupted by Ted trying to attract her attention. He had been fussing around in the back of his vehicle, and wanted to make sure that they each had a liter of water and various other things — preparing for whatever the bush might throw at them. There had been some discussion at UFODD HQ about whether or not Sam and Byron should be armed, but this had been ruled out. "Think of peashooters against Kalashnikovs—a waste of time and not calculated to give the right impression if they *are* ETs," had been Commander Grave's caustic veto.

The three kilometers they had to navigate through the thick forest to point X seemed endless. Sometimes the wiry undergrowth was so thick and tangled that they had to hack through it using their jungle knives. By the time they emerged into a slight clearing, the very spot identified as their destination by their GPS, they were covered in scratches and insect bites. Ted made them roll up their sleeves and trouser legs to check for ticks and leeches, which were oblivious to the insecticide they had liberally sprayed on themselves before setting off.

Sam was impressed by the way his bush navigation had transformed Ted from a monosyllabic watcher to an alert and enthusiastic guide. She realized that his earlier discomfort had nothing to do with them as individuals, but simply to the fact that he was unused to socializing. She could not imagine the boredom and monotony of spending the bulk of one's waking life alone in an observation tower in a forest. Byron remained singularly unimpressed.

Here, deep in the bush, Ted was in his element and able to show off his skills as an experienced bushman. He had been looking intently at the ground in the clearing, carefully brushing aside grass and leaves in places, using a length of stick he had picked up.

"I thought I could smell 'em. Dingoes. Look, that's scat there," he said, pointing at a small piece of dung, and continued to poke around. He bent over to sniff at the base of some of the trees at the perimeter of the clearing. "They mark their territories just like all dogs do," he said. "Quite a few of them in this pack—maybe as many as twenty, I'd say."

"Speak of the devil," he said, suddenly, gesturing at the others to stand still and stay quiet. On the edge of the clearing they could see a group of the native dogs. They kept a wide berth from the trio, but seemed to be searching the ground, sniffing every blade of grass. Ted muttered "Bloody strange, only males in this pack." As if on cue, one of the pack, a large male, turned his head to the sky and howled mournfully. The others followed him in chorus. It was a primeval sound to chill the blood.

« »

Returning via the same route they had come proved easier than the getting in. It had not taken them long to take their readings and search for any signs of physical intervention at the site—but there were no indentations on the ground, no sign of fire or even bent foliage in the surrounding bush. Their instruments similarly showed no evidence of any background radiation.

But both Sam and Byron agreed that there was a faint and indefinable smell within the clearing. The main mystery was what had been upsetting the pack of dingoes. The all-male dingo pack had walked around a particular spot for half an hour as if they were searching for something they had lost. Eventually they wandered off as quietly as they had arrived.

"Never seen anything quite like that," the laconic Ted remarked.

"And there's nothing else you wanted to tell us is there?" Sam probed.

Ted scratched a side burn absently, seemed to hesitate but eventually said "Nope—just a feeling I s'ppose. I know what I saw last night, the light an' all, but today— just them dingoes. Something upset 'em. That's for sure. They were lookin' fer something is what puzzles me the most. There was something strange about that place including that smell I never come across before."

"Any ideas at all on that?" Sam persisted.

Ted chose to stare at a distant view rather than look Sam in the eye. "What do you think happened to their mates? Do you suppose they'd told all the bitches to stay behind while they went on their walkabout?"

They left Ted at his lonely station atop the lookout, thanking him for his guided tour. They explained that the sighting was classified as far as the government was concerned and had him sign a non-disclosure order.

They woke their pilot, who had been taking advantage of the lay-over to snooze, and headed west towards the source of the second sighting that had been identified. It was approximately one hundred and fifty kilometers to the west of the State Forest and only a short trip in their TEC.

"What on earth did you make of that Ted character?" Byron asked Sam on the way.

"I'm still trying to figure out why he was so reluctant to explain what he was thinking."

"Yes, not a great talker and definitely defensive about what he was saying."

"Maybe he felt that whatever it was—it would not be believed if it were to ever get out or be seen by his bosses?" suggested Sam.

"Such as?"

"Maybe he actually did see more than that cone of light he was talking about. Maybe he saw something that didn't add up to him, something he couldn't explain."

"It is more than a coincidence that there should be two sightings here in Queensland roughly a hundred kilometers apart, both relating to possible UFOs, wouldn't you say?" said Byron.

"Yes and there's also that one at Wirrabera. Now how about this for a leap?" Sam continued. "Maybe the first one was responsible for abducting the pups. This second one took the female dingoes. It's why the males were looking so mournful, but I'm suspending my judgment until we've heard what the other sighting people have to say."

"It sure is a leap! Where's the evidence? No-one actually saw pups or dingoes being sucked into a spacecraft did they? That is unless it's the part of the story that both Ted and Sens are holding back. I hope our next call will give us more to go on than that that hayseed," Byron remarked.

"That's a bit uncalled for. I think there's a lot more to him than that. For someone who's never been exposed to ETs, it's not surprising he would keep strange happenings to himself, don't you think?"

"Maybe, maybe not—those guys are often a little touched in the head—the job does it to them," said Byron, tapping his forehead meaningfully.

"I think you underestimate the guy—he'd leave you for dead with his bushcraft!"

"But maybe not in the social skills."

"*You think so*?" said Sam sarcastically, and left it at that.

« »

At the next location reporting a sighting turned out to form part of an immense sheep property, now a horse stud. The Hancock family that owned the property—a man, woman and four children of various ages—were milling around in excitement at seeing their late model copter. The pilot had to fend the children off gently as they pleaded with him to let them aboard.

Sam and Byron saw a man approaching them from across the paddock dressed in protective white clothing including a helmet and face mask. He paused at the gate, took off the gum boots he was wearing and put on another pair of shoes. The Hancocks rounded up their children and moved off a respectful distance allowing him to introduce himself. As he got closer they could see that his eyes were bloodshot and he had an exhausted look about him of someone who had been up all night.

They briefly touched elbows in the standard pandemic greeting originating from the COVID-19 outbreak in 2020.

"Daniel Bell. I'm the vet in charge of this outbreak." Byron and Sam were looking confused. "Hendra virus— we've got three horses infected. I've just had to put one down," he said, solemnly.

"We thought you'd reported a sighting?" asked Sam.

"Oh, that's why you're here. I assumed you were from Health."

"No, we are actually Special Agents attached to a US Based organization which investigates unusual sightings of what are commonly known as 'UFO's'. Your sighting came to our attention and that's why we're here." Sam could not help noticing that Daniel despite his tired eyes and disheveled state was something of a hunk, and felt a wash of sympathy as he smiled sadly back at her.

"Unfortunately this property has three infected horses. I've already had to put down one of them, the other two are also unlikely to survive."

"Can we talk about your sightings, the ones you reported," said Byron, becoming impatient with what seemed like irrelevant chit chat. "Tell us what you saw?"

"I've got some spare sets of protective gear in my 'ute," said Daniel. "We can go to the place where this happened and I'll tell you about it on the way." He walked closer to them and lowered his voice: "I don't want to upset the family with this, they've had enough to deal with losing one horse so far, and the remaining two have a less than 50% chance, I'd say."

They crossed a three hundred meter wide paddock with some difficulty, particularly Sam who was wading through the long grass in a pair of gumboots two sizes too large for her. They finally reached a wire fence and crossed over into a large grove of trees surrounding a clearing.

"This is the place," Daniel said. "Of an evening you can see hundreds of bats roosting in these trees—they go for the figs big time—if you look up you should see them hanging on the branches," he said, pointing to one of the colonies.

Sam had already noticed them, having been brought up in Sydney where it was commonplace to see flying fox bats swarming at twilight, slowly flapping and maneuvering in their ungainly manner of flight.

"I should explain," said Daniel "the reason I'm vet in charge of this outbreak is that I've been doing research on Hendra to nail down exactly how the horses get infected. It's generally been assumed that the horses ingest bat droppings, or maybe the bats bite them, and I've been checking whether this is plausible or something else is happening, but…"

"Is this at all relevant to the sightings? I'm sure that Hendra's your baby, but do we need to know this?" interrupted Byron, with a brashness bordering on downright rudeness brought on by a long morning and lack of sleep.

Daniel stared Byron down, taking his time to answer. He wasn't about to put up with this kind of arrogance after a long night without sleep himself. "It's very relevant, mate, and I suggest that you shut up and listen." Byron flushed and did as he was told. It was obvious to Sam that he needed to be more careful with his manners. The vet looked like he'd been ready to deck him.

"Last night, I was watching the bats in this colony doing their night manoeuvres as part of my research. I had plenty of time to do this as I was tending to the sick horse just over there." He pointed out the body of the horse in the long grass behind the fig tree, which until this point they hadn't noticed.

Rodney Jensen

"There was a formation of about fifty bats above this clearing—they were circling around for some reason, maybe they'd picked up a low-level air up-current to gain altitude. But then suddenly there was this spotlight coming from above—it showed each of the bats in clear profile. But instead of flying away, as I would have expected, they continued gently spiraling upwards—it was like one of those images you see of tornadoes in Midwestern USA, sucking things up in the vortex—only this was a silent movie. The bats were undisturbed; they just kept going up, the light went off and they were gone."

"What do you mean, 'gone'?" asked Sam.

"When the light went off they were gone. I've never seen anything like it before."

"Could it be that the light blinded you and by the time you'd recovered your night vision they had simply flown off or out of range?" asked Byron, more politely this time.

"I don't think so. They were gone. That's for sure. I know what I saw."

There was no shaking his certainty on this.

On the way back to base, Sam felt it was her duty to tell Byron exactly what she thought of him. She started off, by remarking: "That was a really delicate method of information-gathering with Daniel. Just where did you learn such skills?"

"Who the fuck do you think you are?" blustered Byron.

"You carry on behaving the way you did with that vet and I'll be reporting your incompetence for field work. I can't work with someone like you."

"You do what you like, Ma'am. The feeling's mutual."

There was a frosty silence in the TEC the whole way back to base.

CHAPTER 7 Tracking down Marshall

r. Petersen…Mr. Petersen! The voice, becoming more and more insistent, penetrated the blurry fog, and he slowly regained consciousness, peering into unfamiliar surroundings. Sens focused first on the metal rail that his arm was draped over. He moved his head slightly and recognized that it belonged to a hospital gurney.

"Mr. Petersen, can you hear me?" The voice belonged to a young Asian woman dressed in white, with the headgear of a nurse. She had an anxious, compassionate expression on her face.

"Where's Marshall?" asked Sens blearily—his first thought, and then, "what am I doing here?"

"You have caught a tick," the woman said. "And who is Marshall?"

"Marshall is my dog—where is he?" Sens was trying to lift himself out the gurney but the effort nearly caused him to black out again.

"Please do not try to get up, you are very sick and it will take hours before the antidote takes effect. You must rest and I will try to find out what has happened to your dog."

"How did I get here?" Sens asked.

"You called an ambulance and you were found beside the road in your ATV—don't you remember?" she said.

Sens had no recollection of calling an ambulance, and in any case his holo was out of range, so he felt bewildered by what she was saying—even more than his scrambled brain was already feeling. He felt anxious and helpless about Marshall, but assumed that maybe, under the guidance of the Nest, he had decided to make himself scarce while the ambulance was around. As these thoughts circled around, he drifted back to sleep and it was several hours before he came to again.

By this time there was bright sunlight streaming through the hospital window, and Sens woke with a slight headache but feeling much better than he had the night before. Sens was an impatient man at the best of times, and when a white-coated doctor finally dropped by to see how he was progressing, he was feeling frustrated and irritable.

The doctor asked him to describe his symptoms, shined a light in his eye and tested his blood pressure. "You are one of the few cases we get of ticks having serious side effects on humans. It's more common with older people and those with allergic tendencies. Have you been out bushwalking or something?" he asked.

"Not exactly, apart from a couple of stops on the way here. I suppose that might have been where I caught it." He paused a moment before remembering his main concern. "But I'm fine—I want to get out of here. I need to track down Marshall."

"Marshall?"

"Yes Marshall—my dog—he probably saved my life."

"I'm afraid I don't know anything about Marshall," said the doctor.

"But I told the nurse," said Sens.

"There's no mention of it here," said the doctor scanning the notes on Sens' clipboard, "but then I don't suppose there would be," he said in an offhand tone. "What did you mean about saving your life?"

"I think he was responsible for an ambulance finding me," said Sens.

"I don't think so," said the doctor. "The notes here say that the authorities received an emergency call from someone. Possibly a passing car. We don't know who it was because they rang off before giving their name; and in any case, what would your dog have to do with calling an ambulance?" he asked amused.

Sens paused for a moment thinking what to say: "Perhaps he stood by the ATV and that attracted someone's attention. I know who it was," said Sens.

"Do you mean the caller?" asked the doctor.

Sens nodded.

"How so?" asked the doctor, sounding more intrigued.

"I can't really explain," said Sens becoming agitated. "In any case it's not relevant. I want to get out of here and find what has happened to Marshall."

"You're not fit to leave here at the moment," said the doctor. "You have just spent the best part of twelve hours in semi-consciousness. I'd like to keep you here for another twenty-four hours at least to make sure there's no recurrence. You might not be so lucky next time."

« »

Sens was not a happy man for the next couple of days. He was unused to being confined to a hospital bed and ordered around by the matron the moment he wanted to do anything remotely active. "You've just got to stay in bed until the doctor gives you the all clear," she insisted, making Sens feel like a child.

The 'all clear' came eventually, and Sens, still worrying about Marshall, could not get out of the building quickly enough in case they changed their minds. But as he was heading through the exit door another thought came to him. He turned on his heel back to the inquiry counter, to ask where the local dog pound might be. He was given directions to the Shire Council offices.

« »

It took Sens a while to find the Shire Council because it was not clearly signed, and shared the same building with other government offices. The woman at the reception desk told him, "If they have him, he'll be in the holding place in Anson Street, next to Renshaw Oval. It's a bit of a walk from here." She pulled out a map and pointed to a place on the other side of the town. "I'd call them to check they've got him first if I was you." Then without waiting, she picked up her holo and selected an icon.

"Reception from Shire offices here," she said, "got a gentleman who's lost his dog." She was staring at Sens as she said this. "Okay, I'll put him on," she said, and handed over the holo.

Sens described Marshall to the man on the screen.

"Shit!" the man exclaimed, "there was a dog like that come in here the other day, but he's gone. I don't know what happened to him."

"What do you mean he's gone?" said an agitated Sens.

"Look, it wasn't me on duty yesterday. It was me Rostered Day Off. You'd better talk to Jimbo—he was on that day. He'll be back in tomorrow. We're open at 8.30."

With that he was gone.

Sens was left holding a holo with a blank screen. He handed it back to the receptionist who had been taking it all in, her forehead wrinkled in concern.

"Don't worry, I'm sure your dog'll be right. Those animal rights people spread a lot of lies about us," she said.

"What do you mean?" asked Sens. The woman shifted in her seat uneasily, realizing that she had probably said too much.

"Oh! Well, see, there's this website they put out; claims Bourke's one of the worst killing pounds in NSW—they call themselves 'Terminal Pets' or some such name. It's all bullshit but," she added. "They never euthanize, unless it's a killer dog. Most dogs they hold for two weeks minimum. So you'll be right—don't worry."

Her soothing words had completely the opposite effect on Sens, who could hear from her voice that she didn't really believe a word of what she'd been saying.

« »

After leaving the council, Sens realized that getting his ATV back should be his first priority. But with one main street and few car rentals available, it took him nearly an hour before finding one unattended, a kilometer from where he'd started. He set the controls on manual and drove back out along the Brewarrina Road.

He found his own ATV just as he'd left it, and before doing anything else, made sure that it was still going. Then he entered his ID into the hired car and was charged what seemed like an outrageous amount for the thirty kilometers or so he had travelled. He angrily punched the auto-return setting, and the car set off, leaving him to follow after it, back to Bourke.

He checked into a small motel, and then spent the rest of the day taking a look at what the town had to offer. Without Marshall, he felt desolate, and there was little to spark his attention except for an ancient steam pump that had been restored and occupied center stage in a museum beside the Darling River.

He spent the evening in his room, idly watching endless news of the pandemic unfolding around the world. In his depressed state, it was difficult to take in the scenes he was watching. He went to bed early and spent a restless night, hoping against hope that the dog pound would have better news for him the following day.

Rodney Jensen

Sens was at the pound long before opening time, but even when the pound was supposed to be in business there was no sign of life. Sens had to wait an anxious three quarters of an hour before the door of the pound office finally swung open.

Sens found himself staring at a large man in a loose-fitting sleeveless vest, shorts and elastic-sided boots. His tattooed arms, ponytail, and hair tightly drawn back from his sweating forehead made him look more like a biker than a Council manager.

"You the guy who called about a dog yesterday?" the hulk asked. He had a defensive air, the way he was standing with both hands resting on the edge of the counter.

"Yes," said Sens—"You're 'Jimbo'?"

"That's me," he said. "What kind of dog?"

"A Kelpie-Labrador cross. He's black, with white paws, and he's seven years old," said Sens.

The man thought for a moment, and scratched his chest uneasily. "Was he tagged?" he asked.

It was Sens' turn to feel uneasy. "I can't remember," he said. "I've had him a long time, given to me by a friend who was heading overseas. Marshall was less than twelve months old when I got him. My friend said something about needing to get him tagged at the time but I forgot to follow it up."

"See, it's like this," said the man. By this time his hands had moved off the counter and he was standing with his arms crossed. "We had a dog in here the day before yesterday. Sounds just like the one you described. It was picked up by Council's control officer—he found him wandering along the main road from Brewarrina. When we checked him out there were no sign of a tag. We thought he might have come in from one of the properties round here, since he looked like a sheepdog. I made a couple of calls but no one had reported one missing."

"Then where is he?" asked Sens.

"That's it," said Jimbo, absently scratching the back of his head. "You see, when a dog comes in here and isn't tagged, the chances are he won't be claimed, and it's Shire rules to euthanize them after two weeks. He was a gentle pooch and I've a mate I play league with whose daughter lost her dog only a week ago. It was run over, like. They never found who did it," he said.

"You've given him away!" shouted Sens, "I don't believe it!"

"Look, mate, I thought I was doing right. I found him a good home—the chances are he wouldn't be claimed and we'd have had to euthanize him. If you'd had him tagged as the law requires this wouldn't have happened." Jimbo had his arms crossed again and was staring at Sens with a take it or leave it expression.

"Who's this person you gave him to?" said Sens, his voice rising.

"I don't want you making trouble, mate," replied Jimbo. "The dog's gone and there's not much more I can do to help."

"We'll see about that," said Sens, and stormed out of the office.

« »

Sens thought that a family whose father played in the local rugby team and had their dog run over recently should not be too difficult to track down.

At the Shire library he scanned through the last three weeks' editions of *Nyngan Examiner* online to discover an article about someone yet to be identified who was responsible for running over Matt Howard's pet dog, Matt being the Captain of the 'Bourke A-League Rugby Team'. There was a photograph of him and his tearful daughter, Virginia, aged nine, holding a bunch of flowers. Further searching showed that Bourke's rugby team would be playing on their home field the coming Saturday. He also uncovered Howard's address at a property located just thirteen kilometers out of Bourke.

Sens first thought was to try contacting Matt direct using his holo. Then he worried that a call from a complete stranger would arouse suspicion at the very least, and at worst, absolute refusal to talk any further.

Instead he decided that his best strategy was to catch Matt unawares after the next match, explain his situation and hope that the man would have the decency to give his dog back to him.

During the three days until the match Sens spent anxious hours wandering around the main streets of Bourke hoping he might catch sight of Matt with Marshall somewhere, perhaps in the shopping center, but to no avail.

On one occasion a police van pulled alongside him, a uniformed officer leaned out of his window. "We've noticed you around quite a bit mate. What are you up to?"

Sens thought for a moment, wondering what to say. "I've just been looking for my dog."

"Your ID please?"

Sens produced his license. The policeman keyed his details into the van's dashboard monitor, and looked intently at the screen, before handing the license back to him.

"Where're you staying?"

"The Darling River Hotel."

"I'd be watching out if I was you. We've got a few bad people round this place. It's only a matter of time before you get yourself mugged. Take my advice and leave your details with the Pound. They're far more likely to find your dog than you are."

Sens thanked him for his advice, resisting the urge to tell him exactly what he thought of the Pound as the policeman sped off.

Rodney Jensen

Come the day of the match, Sens headed for the local football field and sat down in the top row of seats in the grandstand. He found it difficult to concentrate on the match; he was so wound up about the coming confrontation. As it turned out, the home side got a trouncing by the Narrabri Raiders.

The hooter signaled Bourke's ignominious defeat and Sens mingled with the crowd as the downcast Bourke team met a mixed reception from their families and supporters. Sens waited while the Captain and his team headed for the changing rooms. Half an hour later they began to emerge in twos and threes.

At last Matt came into view having changed into jeans and a matching blue vest. Close up he was a tall muscular man with tattooed shoulders, a prominent jaw and long dark hair tied in a ponytail. He swaggered slightly and radiated aggression. His Akubra and elastic sided boot marked him as farmer and a thirsty one as he appeared to be heading to the nearest pub to drown his sorrows with his mates.

Sens plucked up courage and walked directly in front of him, introducing himself brightly, trying to sound like a supporter.

It was as if he wasn't there. Matt looked straight through him like he was an annoying blowfly. "Yeah, what?"

"I've come about my dog. The Council Pound gave him to you by mistake. He was picked up by the Pound while I was in hospital after I was involved in a road incident. But he is my dog and I really want him back. I've had him for years and…"

Matt rudely interrupted him. "No way mate. He's my dog now and I'm not about to give him away."

"But he is my dog and the council had no right to give him to you. I want him back, now."

Matt turned to one his team mates beside him. "Some people just don't get it do they?" His friend nodded.

Matt turned back to Sens. "Now listen here, I'll say this once and if you don't bugger off, I'll fucking deck yer! The dog is mine and I've got the papers to prove it. It's for my daughter who lost her dog a week or two back. There's no way that I'm goin' to give you Roundup. No way! You shouldn't had him un-tagged and lost him in the first place if he meant so much to you!"

With that he turned and stormed off. Sens hurried after him trying to remonstrate, but his equally aggressive teammate intervened.

"You heard what Matt said. He's not gonna give you back his dog and there's no point in trying to make him change his mind. If I was you I'd piss off while you can. If you try to make something more of this you'll be the loser I can tell you!"

Sens knew when he was beaten and slowly walked back to his hotel room, tears running down his cheek.

« »

Rodney Jensen

After a restless night in his basic and depressing hotel room, Sens decided that any further attempt to convince Matt with reason or even to bribe him with money would be futile. Perhaps he could offer the family another puppy in return, but that seemed unlikely to work either. The only other way that he could think of was to steal Marshall back, and that didn't really appeal, it was not something he would have normally even contemplated...but he was desperate. What other choice was there?

With some reluctance and trying to be as nonchalant as possible, Sens asked several people directions to Matt Howard's property. He knew that this could have repercussions and anyone he asked might well be wondering what he was after. His cover story was that he was scouting rugby players for other teams. The risk remained that once the police started asking around about a stolen dog, anyone asking about the Howard Property might be seen in a different light. As it turned out, Matt was well known around town and several people gave him vague directions to Matt's farm. He made a check with the main location/mapping system on his holo but could only get a *location not identified* message. But he decided to try and wing it from the vague information he had been given.

Sens waited until late in the evening before setting off in search of the place. His attempts led him along obscure tracks off tracks, with an absence of any signs or property numbers. At one point he was completely lost. He made many false turns and frequently had to backtrack before finally discovering the right place. In the end he came across it almost by accident, spotting an open-ended kerosene drum masquerading as a letter box, with a sign that read: **Howard** *Springdale* **Lot 481**.

It was close to midnight, and the sky was moonless and dark. From the road he was able to make out a deeply rutted gravel track, surrounded by scrub stretching out over a flat landscape. The track was lined with an avenue of ragged gum trees, making it even darker than the surrounding paddocks. Sens drove on a couple of hundred meters past the gate, parking under one of the trees at the side of the road to make it less noticeable. He walked back to the gate, undid the chain and hoped that no one passing would see him entering. Anyone *walking* rather than driving up to a country property at that time of the night would definitely appear suspicious.

He walked stealthily along the track, nearly breaking his ankle on one of the deep ruts, before reaching a turn that opened out into a completely cleared area containing a large ATV parked beside a homestead. It was a decent sized building that looked recently built, with verandas all around and a steep corrugated iron roof.

As Sens reccied the homestead, he experienced his first lucky break—he could make out Marshall straining at a chain close to a kennel at the back of the property. He had his nose in the air, wanting to run over to Sens, who had stopped frozen in his tracks, hoping beyond hope that no one would hear the sound of Marshall's chain clinking and come out to check what was going on.

Sens softly approached Marshall, staying as much as he could in the shadows of bushes and trees. Marshall was whimpering with excitement as Sens undid the chain. He stroked his ears to calm him down, put him on a short lead he had brought for this purpose, and started back the way he had come. So intent was he on making sure that Marshall would keep quiet, he completely missed seeing a fallen branch in front of him. He stumbled and fell headlong onto his face, grazing his knees and elbows. He was shocked and winded rather than seriously damaged. After a few moments he was able to scramble to his feet, but the noise must have alerted someone inside the house. A light came on above the front door and he could hear it being unlocked.

"Who's there!" a voice barked.

Sens could hear a man's steps crunching on the loose gravel behind them, and immediately pulled Marshall off the track into the trees and scrub. Then in the darkness they nearly tripped over a large wombat, busily engaged in burrowing a tunnel into the earth. Marshall started barking furiously, and the startled animal bounded away from them, back onto the track. The man, alerted by the sound of barking and the frightened wombat, was shining a torch down the track. Its crisscrossing beam caught a flash of wombat as it fled from the light, crashing through the undergrowth on the opposite side of the gravel. Sens had found a largish tree to hide behind, and lay prone on the ground, completely still.

The sound of Marshall's barking and the glimpse of a startled wombat convinced the man that something was amiss. He swung his torch into the scrub from where it had erupted and began approaching the spot where Sens and Marshall lay in hiding.

Sens, meet me down at the entrance gate in ten minutes, said the Nest, as Marshall sprang into action, barking furiously and racing past the man, back up the driveway.

"Come 'ere, you bugger!" Matt shouted. Sens watched from his hidden position as Matt ran after Marshall at an impressive pace determined not to give up easily, despite the distance between him and Marshall growing by the second.

As they reached the homestead, Marshall seemed to be slowing. He loped up to the paddock beyond the garden and then leapt over the barbed wire fence as if he had miraculously regained his youthful vigor. Matt, huffing and puffing after him, was sure he had him, his anger and rugby stamina spurred him on and he was determined to catch the dog even if it killed him. Marshall had slowed down to a walk and was infuriatingly close to Matt when he suddenly changed course and began circling around a dormant flock of sheep. It was as though someone had activated the whole flock with a cattle prod—the sheep came to life in unison, rushing to form a dense pack around Matt, making it almost impossible for him to move.

Matt, completely hemmed in, cursed and was forced to climb on top of the closely pressed and seething backs of the sheep. He finally tumbled to the ground as he reached the edge of the flock, discovering that Marshall had completely disappeared into the darkness. He searched fruitlessly for a good twenty minutes before giving it up as a bad job and going back to his house, muttering profanities as he went.

He poured himself a slug of locally distilled whisky (by another teammate) to wind down before going back to bed, noting that none of the rest of his family had even stirred from their deep slumber. It was not simply the frustration of having lost his dog. He was convinced someone must have let him off his chain. But what worried him most was how the dog had so effectively manipulated his sheep to prevent him following. In his entire life as a pastoralist Matt had never seen anything like it. The dog had an uncanny ability with sheep that defied any rational explanation. He resolved not to leave the matter there.

« »

Sens, following the Nest's instructions, waited a full ten minutes in his hiding place after the sounds of Matt chasing after Marshall had receded to silence. He stealthily picked his way through the scrub and tiptoed his way back to the entrance gate. Marshall was there waiting for him. He was sitting on his haunches, his ears up, and his tongue lolling out of his mouth in a rhythmic pant, his eyes fixed on Sens with his expectant look.

You've taken your time finding me, said the Nest. *We'd better get out of here. It won't be long before Matt tries checking down here. He is not a man to be trifled with.*

They hurried back to the ATV and drove off. Eventually Sens found his way onto the main road to Dubbo having decided he had had quite enough of Bourke. There were too many people who had helped him find his way to Matt's place, and he wanted to avoid being arrested for trespass and theft.

CHAPTER 8 The noose tightens

Aweek after Sens and Marshall had left the scene, a report of the theft had filtered through the Bourke Command information system and relayed to UFODD under a long-standing agreement of intelligence sharing. The file included a copy of an interview of Matt Howard that had appeared in the Nyngan Examiner Online with the headline 'Howard's second dog misfortune'.

Sam was the first to read the report. "Here's our friend Petersen again with his mysterious dog. Take a look at this!"

Byron scanned through the document. "I think we need to interview this Howard as a priority, it's a pity we didn't get this earlier, Petersen and his dog could be anywhere by now."

"That's true, but it might not be as difficult as you think. If he stayed in Bourke let's find out where and see if they have any idea where he may have gone. If he's now in a hotel or motel in this region we can also run checks."

"What if he's found somewhere private to stay in?" Byron pondered.

"Then we'll just have to wait until he and his dog come to our attention again. Could you speak to the police about this? They may take more notice of you than me. If there are any further reports we want them ASAP Top Priority."

"OK, I'm on it," said Byron sounding pleased to be asked.

« »

Byron's contact in Bourke Police reported that Petersen had been admitted to Bourke District Hospital unconscious and suffering from tick bite. After a call to the hospital admissions, the two were at the grounds less than two hours later. "That's quite a place for such a small town," remarked Byron as they viewed a group of modern looking single storey buildings spread right across the head of a long driveway surrounded by expansive lawns and generous parking bays.

"State's putting a heap of money into places like this where the majority of voters are poor and unhealthy," Sam observed. "I'm just hoping to find their records are up to scratch as well."

The admissions staff were keen to help the inquiry and arranged for Sam and Byron to interview the nurse who'd been in charge of Petersen.

The nurse did not have to think much before saying, "It was the doctor in charge who referred him to our consultant psychologist via video link.

"Why did the doctor do that?" Sam asked.

"I'm not supposed to talk about our patients unless you're family," she said.

"That's OK, we have clearance and you can tell us what it was that worried you about him," said Sam, showing the woman her holo with an official looking form signed by the Hospital's General Manager.

"Well, almost the moment he came to after his tick bite, he wanted to know 'where Marshall was'."

"And that's his dog?" The nurse nodded.

"When I told him that we knew nothing about Marshall, he wanted to know how he had landed up here in the first place, and I explained someone had called an ambulance."

" 'That must have been Marshall', he told me. But he was still not himself and I thought he must be dreaming. As he got better he told me a lot about Marshall and was really worried about what had happened to him. He obviously doted on his dog, He told me that Marshall was his best friend, kept him company after his wife died, and that they talked a lot to each other. I really think he believed that his dog had somehow contacted the hospital and probably said as much to the Doctor."

Dr Majid Biriani, the hospital's clinical psychologist, actually based in Liverpool in South Western Sydney, was in his early thirties with prematurely thinning black hair. He had heavy framed spectacles and was wearing a smart jacket and tie. He seemed quite used to working remotely and got straight to the point.

"Yes I remember Petersen clearly. In my experience people like him need special attention. Sometimes their delusions can be a threat both to themselves and others."

"Delusions?" Sam queried.

"Yes, one in particular. But my problem is that I am bound to maintain client confidentiality."

"The hospital has granted us clearance for this and you can discuss your patient with us as though we are fellow practitioners working on his case. I'm sending you a copy of the clearance."

Sam was tapping her foot with impatience as Biryani downloaded her clearance and read its contents line by line as though his life depended on it. Then looked up a separate file, "OK that puts me in the clear I think," he muttered finally. "Yes I talked with Petersen quite recently and thought he was borderline for needing to spend more time with me to help with his condition."

"What condition?"

"His delusion that his dog actually talks to him and can do things that humans do that in reality no dogs are capable of."

"Like he was able to call an ambulance?"

"Precisely. But that was the only instance that was particularly remarkable. In the end I put it down to acute anxiety about his dog's whereabouts. And other conversations he referred to I put down to a condition that's found in cases of early dementia."

"Apart from those specific conversations, would you say that there were other signs of that condition?"

"No, and this I have to admit is the strange thing. In all other respects I found Petersen to be intelligent and aware of what is going on around him. But there is one thing that I should add…" Biriani paused as though deep in thought. "There were several instances when he seemed about to say something and then stopped himself continuing. I was sure he was holding something back, but none of my questions led him to reveal what he was hiding."

"Is the man dangerous?"

"No I don't think so. I would not have recommended his release from hospital otherwise."

"Thank you for your assistance with this Dr Biryani, you have been very helpful."

"I suppose that you are not going enlighten me any further about your inquiry?" He faced the camera with an inquisitive look.

"We're sorry Doctor but we also have our protocols and this matter is confidential."

As the two drove away from Bourke District Hospital, Sam turned to Byron.

"Well there's your evidence that Petersen and probably Marshall need to be brought in for questioning. Petersen's dog was front and center when those pups went missing in Wirrabera. And strangely, there have been dingoes involved in the Baracoola sighting as well.

« »

"This looks like the place" Sam announced as she caught sight of the sign on the gate of the Howard Property. She undid the chain and Byron drove through. As they progressed along the narrow gravel driveway up the hill in their ATV, Sam wondered whether her partner was going to alienate this new informant as he had others. She hadn't worked out whether he was like this in his home country or it was just that he didn't feel comfortable with Australians.

"Byron, can we agree that this time I am going to conduct the questioning? I want you to record our interview with Matt and restrain yourself from commenting on what he's saying. Given the sensitivity of what I've already heard, I'd far rather he doesn't know that we are taking it seriously. So please, play it cool. We will make it that you are just the camera person as far as he's concerned, OK?"

Sam had come up with the idea of video recording their interviews as one way of keeping her partner occupied and less intrusive with their interviewees, as well as making a better record of actual witness sightings. Byron clearly wasn't happy, but nodded agreement.

Matt was waiting outside on the verandah, happy that someone had taken his complaint seriously. He immediately suggested showing them the places where Roundup had been chained and the sheep paddock where he'd been hemmed in by the flock. Sam was primarily interested in yet another case of a disappearing dog, but she was happy to see everything that Matt was willing to show them.

Byron cooperated by staying in the background, quietly filming everything including some break-away footage of the wide paddock surrounded by gum trees and a large flock of merino sheep contentedly grazing in the shadier spots. He was becoming more and more in love with this sparse and spacious landscape.

"Was there any damage or any other items taken in the break-in?" asked Sam, beginning her interview in a neutral voice.

"No damage, just the flaming dog. Bloody useless watchdog he turned out to be," said Matt bitterly.

"He didn't bark at all?" asked Sam.

"No, that's the strange part—I heard some noises outside, got up and checked along me driveway. It was some time after that I found that he'd been let off his chain. He couldn't have done that himself, but there was no barking until I was halfway along the track and spotted a wombat running across in front of me, and then here he comes barking like all get out, races right past me and up to me paddock. I run after him, but by the time I get to the paddock he's gone." Matt had carefully omitted telling them about Sens as he didn't want ownership of the dog to be disputed.

"And you're sure that he didn't escape by himself. Slipped his collar or something?" asked Sam.

Matt took a moment to reply. He was finding it difficult to suppress his impatience with the stupidity of the question as he saw it. "Like I said, someone must have unclipped his chain. There was no collar left behind, because me bloomin' dog was still wearing it. You ever heard of a dog unclipping its own lead?"

"That is strange," agreed Sam, struggling to overcome her embarrassment and stay focused. "It almost sounds like an inside job to me," she said. "Do you have anybody else working for you that knows about your property and your dog?"

"No, but like I said, we'd only had him a few days."

Matt led them to the kennel and the chain where his dog had been kept, demonstrating the only possible explanation of his dog's escape was that someone had unclipped his chain. They continued their inspection of the property to see if there were any signs of break in or footprints, to confirm what Matt had already told them. "There are no footprints—I've had a good look myself— the ground's too hard to show anything obvious."

As the conducted tour was completed and Matt was leading them back up the driveway, Sam glanced meaningfully at Byron, drawing a finger across her lips to remind him to keep his thoughts zipped.

"I have to be honest with you, Matt," said Sam "I'm not hopeful that we're going to get lucky with this one, since we don't really have a lot to go on. Is there anything else that you haven't told me about the dog—anything that you can think of that might help us to track him down?"

Byron was still filming Matt as he scratched his head, staring back at the camera, clearly looking uncertain whether to continue. It was obvious that there was something that he was unsure about. "There is something," he finally admitted. "I didn't really want to have to tell you this because it might give you the wrong idea."

"Let's hear it then," said Sam.

"When that dog got into the paddock, he did something which still has me 'mazed. I don't know whether you're going to believe this. I know I saw what happened, but I've no idea how he did it."

"Just share what you saw with us," said Byron from behind the camera. "We're used to hearing some very strange things," he said in a deadpan voice.

Matt got a grip on his emotions and continued. "See, the dog had a talent that I wasn't expecting."

"Talent?" repeated Sam.

"Yep, talent. That's what I said. The dog's a fuckin' amazin' sheepdog."

"Kelpie-cross was the description?"

"That's right. They're often good at herding sheep, but I never seen one like this before."

Matt pointed across the wide paddock to the sheep clustered under a belt of shady eucalypts. "We're carrying 2000 head of sheep here, and a dog is a necessity. My mate at the pound knows I need sheepdogs and that was one of the reasons he let me know when this one had turned up. That and the fact that our other one got run over the weekend before last."

"Yes, that's in the police report," said Sam. "But the sheepdog part is all news to us. What's so special about this one?"

"You ever watched good dogs herding sheep?" asked Matt.

"I guess I have, on TV once or twice," Sam admitted.

"Well, what makes a sheepdog good is that they know how to round them up from the rear, where normal dogs just go chasin' the buggers, and they're all over the place."

"Yes, I've seen that," said Sam, growing impatient.

"This dog had to be seen to be believed," said Matt. "That's why I didn't want to bring it up. That night, when I was chasing him, the sheep were all asleep, but he somehow got them all up and bunched round me, like he was communicating with them somehow. He just ran 'round the back of the flock and before I knew it the buggers were all 'round me. It was like they were deliberately blocking me in. I don't know how he did it. Never seen anything like it before."

"Had you been drinking that night?" asked Byron.

"Don't be so fuckin' stupid. I hardly ever drink at home in front of me daughter. I'm telling yer. That's what happened. Believe it or not."

"OK, but I must admit to having great difficulty in believing your story. This is all being recorded and we'll leave this to our superiors to decide," remarked Byron sarcastically.

"You're a real smart-arse," growled Matt. "Do you know how much a well-trained sheepdog like this'd be worth?"

"No idea," said Byron.

"I reckon that dog's worth at least 20,000, maybe more, because he's sure to be a competition winner."

"And you just happened to be gifted him by your mate at the pound. I wish I had friends like that!" Sam remarked.

CHAPTER 9 Pandemic at large

The moment that Sam entered Grave's office she felt awkward. For some reason unknown to her he seemed far from his relaxed self as he impatiently gestured her to take a seat and fixed her with an inquiring stare as he asked, "So what's this all about?"

"I want to request a special 10 day leave pass, Sir."

His reaction was immediate and curt. "What do you mean *leave?* You've only just arrived here!"

Her heart sank. This was not going as she'd planned. She realized she must stay calm and as unemotional as possible. A thought flashed through her mind how she had handled her father when she was much younger when he was being difficult over things that were really important to her. But Graves was a totally different character and used to recognizing when he was being 'managed'. From the little knowledge she had gained of him, she felt the best strategy was to remain calm and reasonable in making her case.

"The reason I need the leave is to visit my mother whom I haven't seen yet after living overseas for more than three years. She lives in an out of the way part of the Blue Mountains where she is vulnerable to looters, and I haven't been able to contact her. I am very concerned. She may be in trouble, may have been having difficulty obtaining supplies, and, of course, she could have succumbed to the virus—that is my worst fear. I must take this time off to find her and bring her back. I want to get her to move to somewhere safe in Bourke close to me."

"And run the risk of infecting this whole base? You must be joking," Graves glared at her. "I have had some reservations about your trips to Wirrabera and South East Queensland given the mounting pandemic risk, but this one is a very different situation isn't it? The Blue Mountains is considered to be part of the Greater Sydney Region and rightly so given population movements within it, and the greater risk of contamination. You will have to cross the current containment lines. I think this whole plan represents an unacceptable risk both to you and to all personnel in this base."

"Yes, I completely understand the risks and have a plan to mitigate them. As you know the incubation period for the virus is quite short—less than a few days. If I'm away for a total of seven days, then within my leave period there would be time after we have left Sydney for any symptoms of the infection to emerge. Of course I will undertake all the tests, beside the normal decontamination procedures, to be certain that I am cleared to resume my duties here.

"I might add Sir, that since I arrived here, with my fellow investigator Byron, we have covered all the high priority sightings and our findings have been recorded. I do not believe that my absence at this stage would impact our program greatly. I will be able to continue with our investigations remotely once I return to quarantine in the Bourke vicinity."

She paused for a moment to let this suggestion sink in before adding another more emotional plea. "And I must point out that I am the only living relative that my mother has. In the current situation it is highly unlikely that there would be anyone else to help her if she needs it."

Graves seemed a trace mollified if not persuaded but responded strongly. "Sometimes, Samantha, our duty to the public must come first. I regard the situation that we are in as being quite similar to war. I'm sure you're aware that servicemen deployed on missions cannot be afforded the luxury of home leave whenever they have some domestic issue to deal with. In your case, you're not even certain that there is an issue. It would be irresponsible of me to agree to this request. It's completely over the top, Samantha."

"Apart from my personal reasons for wanting this leave, there are other considerations," she countered, as though she had not heard a word of his rejection.

"Such as?"

"I have been talking to my colleagues here about our Intel on the pandemic. It appears that due to our isolation, we are relying almost entirely on second-hand accounts of the pandemic situation and have limited knowledge on how best to counter its spread. All we are seeing are a few refugees who have managed to get through the containment lines surrounding Sydney. We know that these refugees pose a risk of spreading the virus and must be quarantined before allowing any social interactions. However, I'm not sure that we or the local authorities fully understand the extent of social distancing requirements and how best to deal with those who have been infected."

"The fact that Bourke is far closer to the states of Queensland and South Australia than it is to the major coastal centers of New South Wales means that we play a strategic role in management of the pandemic. Don't you think we need to be far better informed than we are at present?"

"No journalist or analyst worth their salt would assess events without seeing them unfold before their eyes. My appreciation of this fast-changing situation will prove invaluable. And if I become infected then so be it. Yes, it is a wartime situation—but being at war requires risks to be taken. Regard me as expendable in this instance. Please. I beg you!"

It took Graves an agonizing minute of total silence to contemplate what Sam had said to him. He had not got to the position he held without being able to see both sides of an argument. On the one hand, he supposed that Sam's mother had a better than even chance of already being dead, in which case it would be a futile mission—Sam would be exposing herself to contagion and possibly the entire base if it went undetected before she came back in. But on the other hand, her point about lack of first-hand objective reporting and analysis of the situation was certainly valid, something that had been bothering him for some time. Many of the other UFODD bases in the global network were completely down or crippled, and in a very real sense the eyes of the world were on this base and its ability to maintain an informed watch on the pandemic.

His answer came as a surprise. "Make it fifteen days," he said finally, "and take Byron with you. Ask him to come and see me straight away. I will expect a full and comprehensive report on your return. Good luck."

The expression on Sam's face said it all. Graves waved her out of the office to indicate that the discussion was over. He particularly did not want her to think of him as an easy mark. Sam hurried out, equally determined to hide her glistening eyes, welling up in response to his surprising change of heart.

« »

Sam and Byron's journey from Bourke to her family home in the Blue Mountains had been surprisingly easy since most of the traffic was heading in the opposite direction. Commander Graves was unstinting in his help to reduce risk, having made his decision to support Sam's mission. He allocated an ATV with sufficient reserve energy to cover the journey from Bourke to Central Sydney and back. He provided them with side-arms, food, water and a complete med-kit for emergencies. The ATV was also equipped with a holo-set giving satellite access to the dedicated UFODD frequencies. Then there were the necessary paraphernalia for filming and recording as much as possible of what was happening. Byron commented wryly, "where are we going to put your mother—on the roof?"

"It does have a roof rack. We may need to re-arrange things, but we can think about that later," said Sam.

« »

It had been years since Sam had visited her mother and her family home and the prospect of the meeting filled her with anxiety. She hoped against hope that the explanation for not being able to contact her was simply to do with widespread outages in the holo-network—a common side effect of the pandemic. But she still could not help worrying.

However, as their ATV pulled into the driveway leading to the house, everything seemed as she remembered it years before. The house lay at the end of a long access road some kilometers from Wentworth Falls. It overlooked amazing vistas of the spectacular blue tinted wilderness after which the mountains were named. The mountains stretched north along the immensity of the Jamison Valley as far as the eye could see. Her mother and her late father had enjoyed many happy years there.

Her mother came to the door and greeted them in complete astonishment, having no idea that Sam was back in Australia. Sam momentarily saw her mother as a stranger—an older woman, much greyer than she remembered, and thin—almost skeletal. She felt awkward at first, particularly with Byron present.

Byron was concerned about leaving any stuff of importance outside unattended and left Sam to talk with her mother while he acted as porter. For a few moments her mother busied herself in the kitchen before returning with a tray of tea things. They sat down at a small table. Sam fiddled with a teaspoon while her mother stared at her expectantly.

Sam was still feeling the strangeness of trying to renew what had once been an intimate relationship after a separation of three years. When she had left Australia, her mother seemed late middle aged with relatively few signs of ageing, but now the signs were there, particularly around her eyes and mouth. She was also wearing spectacles with thick lenses hanging from a cord around her neck, another mark of aging faculties. Although time was short, Sam knew that she must finesse her plan very carefully for any chance of success. Her mother was at least as strong willed as she was and would not be easily persuaded to move out of her home to a safer place in the outback.

Instead, their conversation was confined to explaining more about what Sam had been doing without going into too much detail. She also listened patiently as her mother discussed the happenings with the few friends she had left and her bewilderment with the impact of the contagion in Sydney and its surrounds.

The following morning after breakfast Sam asked Byron if he could take a stroll up to the nearest center and assess how exposed her mother's place was to unwanted visitors. It would enable her to continue discussing the real purpose of their visit.

"Mum," she began, "we need to talk seriously."

Her mother simply nodded.

"You must be aware of the pandemic situation. I know that you're isolated here, but you must realize is it's only a matter of time before it will impact on you directly."

"Of course I know about the pandemic. It's on the news all the time. But I'm safe here. Living in the Blue

Mountains has its advantages because we're isolated. Nobody comes down this way. I don't even need to go shopping anymore because everything's delivered…"

"Yes, you are lucky to be isolated from the worst contagion at the moment, and you seem to be coping very well around the house. But how long do you think you can hold out here?"

Her mother looked at Sam in bewilderment. "I thought I had explained this to you, Samantha. Nobody comes down this way at all. It's completely isolated and there's no reason for people to venture down here. You must have noticed that there hasn't been a car going past since you arrived."

"Mum, you're not getting it!" Sam's voice rose. "While you're isolating yourself here in blissful ignorance of what's really going on, the world's falling apart. There are many desperate people out there, and can't you see that a nice place like this will not go un-noticed for much longer?"

"I hear what you're saying Sam, but from the few brief visits I have made recently to the library, for example, it's nothing like that at all."

"Mum, the situation is much worse than you can begin to understand. I've arranged special leave from the place where I've been working and have brought my assistant along to help me move you to a safer place. It will be near to where I'm working, so I can keep an eye on you and keep you safe."

Her mother's expression was bemused. "What do you mean, dear?"

"You're too isolated here. It's the pandemic. There are looters. You must know about this!"

"Oh no dear, there's been nothing like that here. I think I know this place better than you. I feel completely safe and we do have neighbors you know," said her mother.

"Please!" said Sam, beginning to repeat herself in her frustration, "you do not seem to understand how vulnerable you are. Forget about your neighbors, who will have their own problems to deal with, or the police for that matter. Their hands are full, and even if they were able to respond to a call it would be far too late to save you from harm."

"Sam, your father and I chose this spot very carefully for the long term. We're well away from the shopping center and I doubt very much whether any of these people you're so worried about would even find this place or bother me for that matter."

"You're living in the past, Mum—things have changed. It's your isolation that particularly concerns me!" pleaded Sam.

"My dear, there is absolutely no reason for me to move. I'm staying put. You should not have risked your own safety coming here. Now why don't you just relax so we can both enjoy your visit?"

And that was her last word. She was adamant.

CHAPTER 10 Sydney under siege

The next morning Sam woke after a disturbed night's sleep, realizing that they would have to continue the second part of their mission without her mother. Byron, on advice from Sam and for once showing some sensitivity, had stayed well clear of the impasse. Sam knew that once her mother's mind was made up she could not be shaken. Short of tying her up and removing her forcibly back to Bourke, there was little that Byron and Sam could do but to leave her where she was.

Sam was particularly resentful that her personal problems had ended up this way, wasting time that could have been better spent tracking down Petersen and his dog. She vowed that their second commitment to track the pandemic situation in Sydney would justify their journey. Having made their goodbyes and set off on the second part of their journey, down into the sprawl of the Western Sydney suburbs, it was not long before the reality of a city under siege came sharply into focus.

As they were about to cross the Nepean River, they joined a long queue of cars attempting to pass through a main cordon line.

"I suppose we can't get out of doing this? I have a really bad feeling about getting into the heart of Sydney, knowing how badly it's been hit," Byron remarked.

"I'm not wild about it either, but Graves would never forgive us if we don't follow up on the commitment I made. We'd better start wearing our facemasks from now on," said Sam and pulled two out of a car locker.

Rodney Jensen

Many drivers without valid business permits for Sydney locations were being turned back. Others, whose ID implants showed a residential address in the worst afflicted areas of the city, were also turned-back. The security officers were having a very difficult time explaining the rules and directing drivers to refuges, located at Katoomba and other places in the heart of the Blue Mountains, where they could shelter until it was safer to return.

Sam was tapping her foot with impatience as one distraught man in the vehicle immediately ahead of them was remonstrating with the guard on duty.

"My family!" he was shouting. "Can't you understand that I must get back there?"

Sam had been watching as the guard checked the data base on his tablet, turned back to the man with a stony expression and ordered him to make a U-turn and head back the way he'd come. She guessed that the place he'd been heading for had been designated a no-go area and walled off from anyone going in or out, except for health care professionals.

The guard was about to hand the man a leaflet through his window, directing him to the counseling service in the adjacent parking lot, but the man was having none of that. He planted his foot on the accelerator, leaving a cloud of burnt rubber and a scrunch of metal as his vehicle swerved out of the queue, clipping the corner of the one in front. He accelerated down the breakdown lane, only to miss seeing a spiked belt laid down in his path. Each of his tires blew out and he lost control, fishtailing and side swiping other cars, before finally crashing through a safety barrier and ending up on his roof. Other guards sprang into action and dragged him out of the upturned vehicle before his vehicle's energy pack short-circuited, and exploded in a spectacular flash of white heat. The guards dragged him off in handcuffs and threw him into a paddy wagon already crowded with other drivers who had tried to ignore similar orders to turn back.

« »

From the Nepean there were several other checkpoints to cross. The UFODD logo on their ATV gave them unrestricted right-of-passage, although each duty-guard issued similar warnings: that they should not attempt to enter anywhere that was clearly marked as *no-go area*; that they should wear face masks at all times; remain in their vehicle as much as possible; and maintain minimum social distancing of 2.0 meters from other people in any public areas.

The sprawling suburban areas of Sydney in total lockdown brought back memories of the COVID-19 pandemic which had affected their countries in very different ways while they were still in their early teens. The US had fared much worse than Australia whose remoteness and early closing of borders to the rest of the world had minimized the impact of the virus. But the current pandemic seemed to be impacting Sydney at least as much as Byron remembered in the US.

The closer they progressed towards the center of Sydney, the more like a ghost town it became with very few signs of life, streets empty and the bulk of the populace confined to their homes. Some streets were fenced off and occasionally they noticed groups of medical workers clad in complete cover-up clothing, checking for survivors.

While Sam was driving, Byron was recording as much footage as he could, pointing his lens at anything that moved or looked unusual. Sam noticed that Byron had also been spending a lot of time looking at his holo and was obviously puzzled.

"What's up?" she asked him after the third time she noticed this.

"Stop a second and I'll show you," he said.

Sam pulled over and Byron selected a three-dimensional aerial view of the territory they were crossing. A red spot was tracking across the sky above them. The holo was indicating that it was actually a drone, approximately 5000 meters above their position.

"This tracking app was provided by UFODD," said Byron. "The idea is that any of our drones can identify us so that we don't accidentally get zapped or whatever. But what is strange about the drones I've seen so far," he went on, "is that they're not ours. They also don't belong to the Australian military or the police as the app also has access to their drone flights"

"Well, whose are they then?" asked Sam.

"No idea," said Byron "but I've come across two or three others since we crossed the Hawkesbury—all unidentified."

"ET again?" Sam mused.

"Could be. If that is who those drones belong to, they seem to be taking a keen interest in this pandemic."

"Or us, perhaps?" commented Sam.

« »

Commander Graves had suggested that they should meet Mike Stanaway, the director of emergency operations, bunkered down at a secure location close to the Old Government House and the surrounding park in Parramatta. Graves had left messages with Stanaway's secretary but hadn't been able to connect directly with him before they left. Sam tried again as they were approaching the command center, only to be told that Stanaway was in a meeting and it would be doubtful he could talk to them.

They finally found the command center and discovered that Stanaway had left instructions for them to be processed. They were required to avert contamination risk by lengthy showering and irradiation. Clad in fresh white protective clothing and masks they were admitted into the control room. It was immediately apparent that the scale of the problem affecting Sydney was beyond control.

"We're here to see Commander Stanaway," began Byron, finally getting eye contact from someone staring at a holo-image.

"Have you an appointment?"

"We wouldn't be here if we didn't!" Byron's impatience was showing.

"He's got his hands full at the moment, as I'm sure you're aware. The best I can do is send him a holo-text to let him know you're here. Please take a seat," the man said.

As Sam and Byron retreated to the seating area it was as though they had become part of the furniture. It was not helped by the fact that their protective clothing made them look much the same as everybody else. From where they were seated, they could see people coming and going, many deep in conversation with someone else on the other end of the holo-net.

Time and again they repeated their request to meet Stanaway, getting the same negative response. They could see that their chances of discovering anything particularly useful above and beyond what they already knew were not looking good. It was an hour and a half before Stanaway came over to talk to them.

Having introduced herself and Byron, Sam wasted no time in explaining the purpose of their interview request. "Commander Stanaway, we're here representing the international UFODD Directorate. Our main task has been monitoring extra-terrestrial contacts and part of our research has been to see if we can tie down the current pandemic to ET involvement…"

Stanaway looking bemused at what she was saying, interrupted her in mid-sentence. "My apologies, Agent Mitchell, but I'm needed to sit in on an important strategic decision. You're both welcome to sit in if you like, but I would prefer it if you just listen. Is that okay?" They both nodded.

When Sam and Byron finally got Stanaway to themselves, they wasted no time in posing some basic questions. "What news is there on the vaccine trials? Is there any light in the tunnel? Sam wanted to know.

Stanaway paused to reflect for a moment.

"As you probably know, most of the main global centers have labs that were planned long ago to deal with pandemic diseases including agents used in germ warfare. The labs were all well-designed and equipped with back-up power, internal air pressurization and the ultimate possible levels of air filtration. But the work of analyzing this virus has been severely impacted by a total break-down in energy supply infrastructure. We've been hearing nothing from our own labs lately and fear the worst. Similarly we haven't heard any positive news from overseas."

"As far as I know the labs have been trialing a range of likely possibilities, including investigating the antibodies in blood samples from a few cases of people who have not become infected, but I've yet to hear any optimism coming from the labs so far. The messages I'm getting are that it will be at least 12 months before there are any safe and effective vaccines, despite the intense competition to win the race by all the major players."

When Sam asked him whether they had a handle on the infection rate and other statistics that might be useful for preparedness elsewhere, his response was to hold up his hands to stop her midstream. "The pandemic is growing much faster than we have resources to manage. We grab some sleep when we can.' And as for maintaining statistics, we'll be lucky if we are ever in a position to assess its magnitude or its rate of spread," he said.

"Have you any idea why there are drones above some of the infected areas?" asked Byron, completely changing the subject.

Stanaway looked confused. "Drones?" he said blankly.

"Yes, we monitored several on the way here but they're unidentified on our system. We were wondering if you could shine some light on them?" said Byron.

"Not that I'm aware of," said Stanaway. "We do have plenty of satellite imagery, but drones—no. No idea," he said.

Sam, who was following this interchange in the background, nodded her head to Byron, signaling that maybe it was time to go. She could see that they were not going to get anything of much use, and that Stanaway had other things to worry about, much higher on his list of priorities.

« »

Over the next three days, the pair visited four other control centers. In each of these it had been difficult to catch the attention of the officer in charge. The centers were all understaffed and mismanaged without clear objectives or agility to respond to the changing pattern of contagion. Communications between the centers were poorly coordinated and it was difficult to see any coherent pattern of containment emerging.

Sam and Byron knew that they had accomplished little to justify their mission when it came to reporting back to Graves. But their time was running out and they had decided to return to Base feeling frustrated to have observed a crisis unfolding to which there seemed to be no obvious answers. "Wow. Those guys are a waste of space in their little cocoons!" said Byron, for once sounding angry and frustrated.

"I don't think that's fair. You've no idea how much risk they've already been exposed to in managing this situation, how exhausted they must be feeling, and how little support they're getting. They're doing their best as far as I could see," said Sam.

"Well maybe we have to agree to disagree. What I saw was a serious inability to face reality. If they can't see what's happening in front of their faces, then the problem will simply expand even more beyond their control," said Byron.

"As a matter of fact, and I don't want to sound defeatist, but my impression is that it already has. I think it's highly likely that most refugees we're seeing on all roads out of here are already infected," said Sam.

Byron was on the verge of saying something, when Sam lifted up her hand signaling that she was feeling her holo vibrating. She fumbled in the pocket of her suit pulled it out to see the face of her mother at the other end. She was not looking good.

"What's the matter, Mum, is everything okay?" Sam asked, seeing that she obviously wasn't and glad that she had left behind an up-to-date satellite holo with her mother.

"Sam," she sobbed. "Some horrible people have just broken in and taken everything, including my car. I don't know what to do. Are you still in Sydney? Can you come back and help me?"

Sam held back her instant and impatient response before saying: "Hang on a minute, Mum." She turned to Byron, hoping that he would be feeling the same as she was. He put a voice to her thoughts. "We must get her out of there immediately—she's probably lucky to be alive."

Sam, at that moment, could have hugged him for being understanding in such difficult circumstances. Maybe his witnessing more directly the effects of the pandemic on ordinary people in Sydney was softening his brashness and arrogance?

« »

They found Sam's mother waiting for them outside her door. Normally a proud, well-groomed woman and conservatively dressed, she was in disarray, with her hair a mess, no make-up and wearing a worn dressing gown over her night clothes, despite the cold night air. It was as if she had aged 10 years in the short time since they had last seen her.

They had barely got out of their vehicle before she began to unburden herself. "They shut me up in the bedroom," she said. "I could hear them ransacking the house. I locked the door, but all that time I was waiting for them to barge in and hurt me…" Her voice tailed off as she relived her fears, feebly brushing aside the tears that were trickling down her cheeks.

Sam did her best to hug and comfort her, but she was still trembling.

"Finally the noises stopped, and I didn't know what to do," she continued in a choky voice. "I waited and waited. Still there was no sound, so I finally unlocked the door as quietly as I could, thinking that at any moment someone might jump me. But the place was empty. Thank heavens they were gone!"

"You're all right, aren't you?" asked Sam.

"They've taken everything, and I have no food left at all. You were right and I was wrong. I'm really sorry I've been so obstinate, bringing you out all this way."

"You must come with us back to Bourke, you can't stay here," said Sam, as gently and firmly as she could. But her mother's resistance to leaving was gone and she was more than ready to put her home behind her.

Sam helped her mother put some of her most important clothes and keepsakes into two suitcases. They strapped some of their other bulkier provisions onto the roof rack to leave themselves room for her inside the vehicle.

As they drove through the night Sam's mother stretched out on the back seat and fell sound asleep in the relative security of her daughter's presence. The unspoken fear for all of them was whether she might have been infected by the looters. They had donned face masks and shared the driving, making a quick journey to the edge of town as the sun was rising the following day.

Sam had contacted Graves and explained the situation. Graves said they should stick to his original plan and that they must remain off-base for at least fourteen days in case they began to show any symptoms of contagion. He mentioned that he'd been in contact with the State Health Agency to make sure they were all up to speed in identifying symptoms, particularly including elderly personnel like Sam's mother.

Sam promised that she would be sending in her report concerning the spread of the pandemic and implications it had for Sydney and beyond by the end of the next day but indicated that it wasn't good.

"I've always assumed that our UFODD Base is isolated enough. I hope you're not saying it isn't?" Graves wanted to know.

Sam paused before answering. "Based on what we've seen Sir, you may have to re-visit the contingency plan that you have in place."

Graves was silent without directly responding to what she had said. Instead, he changed the subject.

"From my perspective, it makes it all the more imperative for you to remain in quarantine for a full two weeks, and negative tests after that before you can come back here. Fortunately, I've been able to call in a favor with the General Manager of Bourke Council who has kindly put an abandoned cottage a couple of k's out of

Bourke at your disposal. We'll see it's properly provisioned with stores and furniture."

« »

Time hung heavily for the three of them in their isolation. Byron and Sam spent their days researching the pandemic situation and following up on concerns they had identified in Sydney. There were still some newsfeeds who were reporting as it was unfolding in Sydney and other centers which were relaying data via their holo links.

Sam's mother had little to do except settle her nerves by walking around the property and gathering firewood for their primitive open fireplace. It was the only available heating source in the semi-derelict stone cottage but proved completely ineffective at warming the house, barely keeping it much above zero degrees on the freezing days.

One morning close to the end of their fourteen days, Sam had been so engrossed in a report she'd been reading that nothing Byron was saying penetrated, and even her mother's mention that her tea was growing cold fell on deaf ears.

As she put down her holo with an air of finality, she was wearing a curious expression—a mixture of enlightenment and disgust. "Just take a look at this!" Sam's voice sounded sufficiently excited to draw Byron's attention away from what he was reading online. "I've come across something pretty amazing."

Byron picked up her holo, immediately recognizing a 'Highly Classified' stamp and the name 'Commonwealth Security and Intelligence Agency' in the header. The report was in small type, and lengthy.

Byron's curiosity was piqued. "What does it say?" he demanded.

"It never ceases to amaze me what drives some of the extremist movements. There's this group who call themselves 'Final Solution'. It can't be an accident that it's the same name as Hitler's infamous policy for the Jews in the 1940s."

"I think I've heard of Final Solution—are they as disgusting as the Nazis were?"

"Worse, if that's possible," said Sam. "It's not just the Jews or some other racial group they've been trying to exterminate—but a large proportion of the human race. They were strongly advocating plans based on the 'one child policy' in China."

"Jeez, are you suggesting that there might be a link between these crazies and the current pandemic?"

"Yep—that's basically where this classified report leads. There was a mole who was advising US Security who in turn were passing on the info to the Commonwealth Security and Intelligence Agency CSIA. This mole warned that that Final Solution were blackmailing one of CSIA's agents to divulge research that he had access to from a top-secret bio-lab located around here in fact, near to Nyngan."

"And the agent they were blackmailing was?"

It's none other than the leader of the Australian Grazers' Party—Senator John Williams. They were blackmailing him with the information they had on his penchant for child pornography."

"One thing that I have a pretty strong feeling about is that the work of Final Solution and the current pandemic are linked. The disease has great similarity in terms of its symptoms with the HRNX-0 agent the scientists were experimenting with at Nyngan. But Williams is a sideshow as far as I can see. If this report is correct and they did have a successful antidote under development at the same time, that's what we should be concentrating on."

"I think you're right, that's a great lead," said Byron excitedly, "even if it's not exactly part of our remit."

After dinner, Sam's mother had gone to her room early, leaving them in peace. The two were stretched out on the lounge watching the international news, when a message came through on Byron's holo. Sam could see Byron stiffen and a tear roll down his cheek."

"Byron what's the matter?"

"This message has been forwarded on to me from the solicitors who act for my Pop in South Carolina. He's dead and they say that there are expenses to be paid and there is nothing left for me."

"I'm so sorry Byron. Was it the pandemic?"

"I believe so. He was in good health when I left America and he was still in his 70's. But we haven't been good correspondents since I joined UFODD. I've tried once or twice since we've been in Australia but I haven't been able to raise him."

"Can you find out any more about the circumstances of his death from his solicitors?"

"I suppose so. He's been a solitary guy since my mum died. He moved out of our home in Charleston just before I joined UFODD. He was living by himself in an out of the way place in a wildlife refuge near to the coast. I think I might have talked to him twice since then."

"If you like I can write to the solicitors for you. It might be less painful that way?"

"Let it go!" said Byron.

"What's the matter? What aren't you telling me?"

Byron paused and took a sip of the bourbon he was partial too. Finally he looked directly at Sam. "I really don't want to know, Sam. The truth is that we didn't part on the best of terms. I lost my job. He was sure it was my fault, that I wasn't trying hard enough, that kind of thing. Truth be known he had a point! But there was no sympathy any more. He gave me an ultimatum to try for the UFODD post they were advertising although I had told him it wasn't what I wanted. He just didn't care whether I got the post or not. The fact was he'd gone broke and had to shut down our family home, the one I'd lived in most of my life. He'd bought this place on the edge of the wildlife refuge without telling me anything about it. He never invited me over. I haven't seen him since. Now it's too late."

"I'm so sorry. I wish there was something I could do to help."

"Let's just change the subject, that's the kindest thing that you can do. The truth is that the last thing I want to know is that my father has caught the pandemic and died in his lonely retreat without anyone to help him. As you can understand with the current travel restrictions I might be able to leave here for the US but not able to return in the foreseeable future."

"So what do you intend to do then? Would you actually plan to stay here?"

"I have been thinking about that," Byron admitted. "I haven't seen any of your cities yet but I have been impressed by some of the places we've visited, particularly the Queensland Baracoola Forest trip we made. Once we get out of this quarantine I'm intending to talk to some agents about properties around here."

"They would be completely different to what you've been used to in South Carolina. Are you sure about this?"

"What appeals to me is the isolation for one thing. In the current climate, isolation spells security. The other consideration is finances. My dad was pretty well off but he kicked me out when he'd made some bad investment decisions. I don't have a great deal put aside because up to the point when I started the UFODD program I'd assumed I would never have to. Properties around here are not selling for much because there's been a drought and there are no buyers. Even with my small savings I can probably manage a large patch of land with a home on it. Run some sheep or cattle even. It kind of appeals to me."

Sam laughed. "Can't see you in a check shirt and a ten gallon hat trying to muster sheep from the back of a horse. Are you really serious?"

"Deadly. I've been meaning to talk to you about this. I was hoping you might be willing to try it out yourself. Help me run the property and bring your mother along if you like?"

"No other commitments beyond sharing the management of your property? I'm not sure where that would leave me?" Sam felt astonished. *Is this for real?*

"Why not just try it out? It would cost you nothing, but you're someone that I know I can trust. You could help me manage things. And who knows, if things worked out between us we could go the further step. I promise that I would never put you under pressure."

Sam did not know what to say. She suddenly felt that there was more to Byron than she'd given him credit for and resolved that she would be more understanding of his ways in the future. But the prospect of becoming a partner in a new farming venture left her bemused.

PART 2

CHAPTER 11 Political machinations

By 2035, Cobar had several pubs, a scattering of shops and houses, and a floating population of prospectors, miners and farmers. During the past fifty years there had been a series of significant mining discoveries with rich concentrations of gold and other heavy metals. But the lodes had diminished causing the costs of extraction to rise each year before reaching a point of economic loss and inevitable closure of many mines that had been the lifeblood of the region.

The town nowadays serviced its local community rather than global markets. It was a refuge from the pandemic and a waterhole for the many pastoralists whose properties surrounded the town. It was also the home to the 'Cobarbarians', the only motorcycle club in the locality.

On this particular day, in a garage to the rear of a nondescript weatherboard house, the Cobarbarians were holding one of their post rally meetings. Most members were obsessed with Harley Davidson bikes. Many of the members were relics of the past themselves—a high proportion retired early because of mine closure.

Today's ride had been long and extremely hot. Despite the protection of their leathers all looked weather-beaten and parched. They were crowded noisily around the drinks bin, oblivious to the notion of social distancing, downing assorted beers, selected wines and privately distilled spirits. A rapidly growing pile of empties lay in a second bin and the raucous level of laughter signified most were already well over the legal limit for riding.

A less widely recognized aspect of the Cobarbarians was the fact they had a more serious purpose than simply recreational motor cycling. The club had originally been established by a small number of dedicated activists with a broadly socialist left agenda—strongly opposed to the predominant right country party, the Australian Grazers', which had its headquarters in the town. The club's main political aims were to sway public opinion against the Grazers', by keeping the media well informed of their issues. They were not above playing a few dirty tricks. However, their sporadic sorties to change the world had so far achieved limited traction.

Graffiti had been scrawled over large advertising posters and on various public landmarks. During recent elections they had run the trick of pulling oppositions flyers out of letterboxes and replacing them with their own, but this had backfired when one of them was caught red-handed. The bad publicity served only to guarantee the re-election of their most hated candidate, Senator John Williams, leader of the Australian Grazers' Party.

Williams stood for everything the Cobarbarians despised. Landed-gentry status, owner of a huge property, mostly left fallow (but a valuable tax haven to neutralize excess income from multiple dodgy enterprises). The list went on. There was very little to like about the man who had his retinue of toadies and cronies and never had given a thought to the disadvantaged or any of the many rural-environmental challenges.

Only one or two in the media might have been aware that there was more to the Cobarbarians than recreational motorbike riding. But with the heavy fine that had been imposed on the club for leaflet substitution, the group had lost its way and was open for new initiatives.

It was an opportunity for a new feminist with a cause to take over—someone with a stomach for blood and a raging chip on her shoulder. This was none other than 'Ballbreaker', following the longstanding tradition that everyone used nicknames to preserve anonymity. She had chosen this one for herself and wore it as a badge of honor.

On this particular day, it was time for Ballbreaker to make her debut, and she was keen to take on the role of leader referred to as Grand Master or Mistress (GM). Since nobody else was willing to stand, she was elected unopposed for an indefinite term. In this sense it might have been thought that the Cobarbarians were supporters of feminism, although the truth was that the majority of the males in the group were lazy rather than being sensitive new age guys.

The group could not have selected a better target of their political leanings than the hated Senator Williams. Ballbreaker herself had deeper and darker reasons to utterly despise him; reasons which she had chosen not to disclose to other members of the group. Her new leadership role presented a heaven-sent opportunity to get even with him.

Ballbreaker had to scream at full capacity to make herself heard above the noise. "Listen in!" she bellowed, waiting for two men gossiping in one corner to shut up. These two were oblivious to the fact that everyone else had gone quiet, finally stopping when they at last realized they'd been noticed. "You quite finished?" she said in a truculent voice, embarrassing them to the full. "Some of you may have heard that the police are still doing the rounds, asking questions about us." There were sounds of agreement and groans.

"One of my contacts in the media tells me that Williams will be opening the Muldoon Estate next weekend. He thinks it's a pretty crash hot initiative and is hoping to get lots of publicity from it. We're going to be sending him a message that couldn't be better timed." There was silence born of confusion as to what she was on about.

"Rumor has it there are few home truths he'll not be so keen for his voters to see when the next *Examiner* comes out," she said, amongst cheers from the group.

« »

The sun was streaming through the window to the home of Senator JC Williams house in Nyngan. Some years earlier he'd converted one of the shop fronts in the main street to be his Grazers' Party electoral office, reluctantly leaving the management of his family property to a live-in farm manager and his family.

His wife was long suffering and patient even though she was particularly unhappy with the new arrangement, far preferring to live on a large property in relative privacy. Williams kept telling her he was planning to divide his time between the farm and the town center, but his electoral business increasingly made that idea fanciful.

Rodney Jensen

As he was breakfasting after a busy week of official functions, his wife appeared carrying his holo tablet.

"There's something there you might want to take a look at," she said, signaling by her tone that it was serious. She activated the news icon and laid it on the table in front of him. He ignored her and went on eating.

"You really should take a look," she nagged him.

Williams wrenched himself from his rasher of bacon, wiped his mouth with the back of his hand and pulled the tablet towards him. He beamed smugly at the large photograph of himself showing on the screen. He'd been announcing the opening of a new supermarket in Bourke two days before. The public group at the opening was limited to single figures because of the pandemic restrictions. It was, nonetheless, very good media coverage for him. But his eyes narrowed as he looked more closely into the heading above the image.

"Fuck!" he swore, "did you see this, Nicole?"

"That's what I was trying to tell you. You need to do something about it. What are you going to tell your supporters? Surely it's not true that the main contractor for the center is connected to our property company, is it?"

Williams stared at her without answering. His expression spoke volumes. The silence was broken by the sound of Nicole's own holo. She picked it up off the shelf, making sure that it was set to audio only. "He's just here," she said, "I'll pass him over."

Nicole mouthed the words softly *"Sydney Morning Herald"* as she gave him the hand piece.

"John Williams," he said in a neutral voice, and listened carefully.

"No comment," he responded in a controlled monotone, and pressed the cut off button, ensuring that no more calls would be answered that morning. His wife was staring at his stony face, and could tell that he wasn't about to enlighten her further.

"Bastards," he swore under his breath, and walked out into the garden, crashing the door violently after him. His breakfast lay half eaten on the table.

Nicole sat down, picked up the tablet and read the article again. She finally put it down with a sigh. She got up, fiddled with some things on the table for a few moments and then, with new resolve, switched her holo back on again and selected a contact. It was answered after only a couple of seconds. "Andrew, you've got to talk to John—he's got a problem."

« »

Williams' day continued to deteriorate when a police ATV-Wagon drew up outside his residence midmorning. A police officer, looking distinctly ill at ease, knocked at the door to be received by Nicole. She seemed reluctant to show him in when he requested an interview with her husband. "He's pretty busy," she said, holding her ground on the doorstep.

"Tell 'em to piss off." A voice could clearly be heard from the depths of the house behind her.

"Can you let him know that it's the police and it would help a lot if Senator Williams could assist with our inquiries?" said the officer.

"Just wait here, then," Nicole said and went back inside, closing the door after her.

A few moments later, Williams emerged, looking less than welcoming, not relishing the prospect of an interview. "What do you want?" he snarled.

"Senator, I think it would be better for all concerned if we were to have this conversation inside." As he said this, the policeman tilted his head in the direction of a man across the road, walking his dog and stopping to gawp at what was going on.

"Thanks for bringing the Wagon. It's great for my reputation," said Williams.

"Sorry Senator, but there were no other vehicles in the pool. It was the only one left and I felt that this could not wait."

Somewhat mollified, Williams gestured to the policeman to head inside and followed after him, carefully shutting the door behind him. They entered the living area, Williams pointed at the settee and the policeman sat down, fumbling with some papers, including a copy of the *Nyngan Examiner* article.

"Is that what you're here for?" asked Williams.

"Yes and no—probably not what you're thinking," said the policeman.

"Please enlighten me on what I might be thinking," replied Williams nastily.

"Actually, I'm not particularly interested in the substance of this story so much, more as how it might have turned up in the media?"

"That thought occurred to me, too, I've got to admit. In this electorate it's sometimes difficult to work out what drives people to say and do what they do. I've frankly given up trying—it's usually irrational—that's for sure." Williams belched up some stale gas from his half-eaten breakfast, without bothering to apologize.

"Have you got any enemies who have the energy and resources to conduct a campaign of this kind against you? This level of detail amounts to investigative journalism." asked the policeman.

Williams laughed bitterly. "You've got to be joking, haven't you?" he said. "This would have to be one of the most polarized communities in Australia. That means at least half, and probably more than that, have some grudge or other against me."

"What about groups rather than individuals?" asked the policeman.

"I suppose that's a possibility too. There's the loony left; the hanky-wringing greenies; the tree huggers; animal rights; gays; refugee activists—you name it—they're all here."

"Hmph." The policeman grunted, not quite knowing what to say and certainly not wanting to reveal any personal affinity to some of the very groups that Williams apparently so much despised.

"We have a watch on a group you may have heard of, the Cobarbarians, and think they may have been behind this," the police officer said.

"Might well be," said Williams.

"We know they're after you, the question is why."

"It's part of their dirty tricks campaign to stop me getting re-elected, isn't it?"

"I'm wondering if it's that simple. Because someone has gone to quite a lot of trouble to dig up this story. Can you offer any other reason that they may be conducting this campaign? It seems to go beyond simple politics for a small town like this."

Williams scratched the back of his head and shifted in his seat before answering. "I had a falling out with one of their members a long time back," he said finally.

"Do you mean a relationship of some sort?"

"No, not exactly. Look, it's personal and I'd like to leave it that way, if you don't mind," said Williams.

"Well, if you change your mind, here's my contact details. If you do think of anything, please give me a call. We would like to find out more," the officer said, handing Williams a holo-chip.

"I'm not sure at this point," said Williams, with a reserve that was unusual for him. "I'll let it percolate. It could be a can of worms. I'll let you know," he said as he escorted the policeman to the door.

As Williams re-entered his living room, he found Nicole sitting riveted in front of the holo, learning about the mounting casualties from the pandemic. "Turn it off, for God's sake," he snapped, but she ignored him, having long lost patience with his frequent outbursts.

She could not understand why her partner would continually avoid watching the news of the pandemic, something in which he should be showing serious leadership. His recent property dealings were difficult enough for her to comprehend, but it was beyond her wildest dreams that he might be connected in some way with the outbreak.

CHAPTER 12 An interrupted opening

After retrieving Marshall from Matt's property, Sens decided he and Marshall needed to head immediately to Cobar, where his distant cousin Raegan lived, and lie low for a few days. They arrived early in the morning, after stopping briefly for a catnap beside the road. Raegan's house lay close to the former railway station near the center of town and at the intersection of roads leading to the towns of Bourke and Louthe on the Darling River. Sens had sent a holo-text to warn his cousin of the visit and his imminent arrival, and the front door was already open as they arrived.

"Sens, how lovely to see you!" exclaimed the man at the door. "I think the last time we met was when you were a child."

"Yes that's probably right Raegan."

Sens' cousin nodded. "Just call me 'Rae', everybody does, and I prefer it that way.

"I guess I must be a little younger than you," Sens continued, "because I clearly remember you coming to visit us when I was just a little kid and playing cricket in our backyard."

"Yes," said Raegan doubtfully, "I sort of remember that, or maybe I just remember my parents talking about it. But what are you doing out here? Oh, do come in!" he added, realizing that Sens was waiting to be asked.

"Do you mind dogs?" asked Sens, pointing out Marshall.

"Not at all. He's welcome too," said Raegan, stooping to pat Marshall. "Oh, and by the way this is my daughter Meg," Raegan said, as a young woman emerged from the house and was standing behind them. She intrigued Sens as she beamed brightly at him. She seemed part indigenous and a little too old to be his daughter. In any case there was no family resemblance with Raegan's fair hair and skin and her unruly black hair and coffee colored skin.

"I'm not sure what to call you? Uncle? Cousin?" she asked.

"Just 'Sens' is fine. Everyone calls me that."

"You can probably guess I'm adopted, but I've been helping Dad out for a while now, since mum died."

"I don't know what I'd have done without Meg around. When Irene passed away I wasn't looking after myself very well, and she came back home to look after me."

Raegan put his arm affectionately around Meg and she smiled back at him warmly.

"Dad, I think we should let Sens come in and sit down before telling him all our family history," Meg said quietly.

"Okay," said Raegan, "it is all in the family, but what I was about to say was we've both been having our demons, and it suited me at any rate to have Meg move in."

Sens had had never met Raegan's wife. "I'm sorry to hear that your wife..." Sens voice tailed off, already forgetting the wife's name.

"Her name was Irene," said Meg.

"...passed away," Sens continued. "I didn't know anything about her, or you, for that matter. Was it recent?"

"Ten years ago, but it still feels like yesterday," Raegan explained. "She was still young—much too young to die. Breast cancer. She was the love of my life—but she's still here," he put his hand on his chest absently.

There was an awkward silence that followed, leaving Sens decidedly curious to learn more. Meg went off into the kitchen and clattered some cups and saucers onto a tray. Before long she was back and acting as the perfect host, serving tea.

"Are you here to see the opening?" she said to Sens brightly, getting him off the subject of Irene's passing.

"Opening?" Sens looked blank.

"The new Muldoon Group Housing project," said Meg.

"No, I've no idea what that is."

"Well then. That's something we can do to interest you," said Meg. "Every man and his dog will be there. It's a big event around here, although there's a lot of controversy about it."

"What Meg is referring to is the new Indigenous group housing development," Raegan interjected. "The Feds have put something like fifty million bucks into it, aimed at providing better housing for Aboriginal Australian People."

"That's where all our tax dollars are going!" Sens exclaimed but then blushed slightly thinking of Meg's background.

"It was a deal between the Government and the Grazers' Party, in an attempt to win votes from Aboriginal Australians in this area. The local Aboriginal people are not exactly in love with the Grazers' given what's been done to them in the past," explained Raegan.

"Totally turned their back on them," muttered Meg quietly.

"The housing project started a couple of years back and was intended to do something concrete for indigenous people. It's been fast tracked in spite of the pandemic, but the critics are already suggesting the work is substandard and the objective is more about shining a better light on the Grazers' Party than indigenous welfare," Raegan explained.

Sens didn't say anything, not quite ready to engage in political discussion with a perfect stranger (albeit his cousin).

"I've got mixed feelings about it myself, I must admit," Raegan continued. "It's a lot of money and it might do some Aboriginal Australian families a bit of good. But it's a drop in the ocean compared to what's really needed. Personally, I worry that it may turn out to be misguided, in fact I am sure it will."

"If there was any consultation about the project, I never got to hear about it," said Meg. "The first thing I knew was that a contract had been signed with a building contractor nobody had heard of. I've already been hearing complaints that the houses they've built are much too small for extended families."

"No doubt the Opposition will seize on those criticisms," said Sens.

"They're not well represented in this area compared to the Grazers'. But I have been hearing whispers of graft and corruption. Personally I think the money could have been better spent on self-help rather than pork barreling for the benefit of the Grazers'. But I'm going to reserve judgment until I see what they've done. Why don't we all go and take a look—the opening's tomorrow," said Raegan.

« »

The new Muldoon development had a half-finished, raw look about it, with stacks of bricks and timber off-cuts scattered around. The concrete pathways were roughcast, and the planter beds sparsely planted with tube stock and covered over with red pine chips. The new houses were sited in small groups, as though some idealist in the government assumed this might generate better social harmony. The houses themselves were designed in a country homestead style, with corrugated steel for roofs, well insulated wall panels, and wide cantilevered verandas providing much needed shade from the searing sun.

What had most attracted Sens' and other visitors' attention was the centerpiece of the estate, a thirty meter high services tower, which everyone was already calling the 'Pah Tah'. The tower was designed to provide centralized services for all the houses. It had advanced solar panels for electricity, hot water and air conditioning, satellite dishes for holo-net comms and storage tanks for both hot and cold water supply. There was also a neighborhood-scaled packet plant to desalinate and purify brackish artesian water.

Beneath the tower, and less well publicized, was an advanced water treatment system that turned sewage and wastewater into separate supply lines for potable water (for drinking, cooking and washing) and irrigation water for the gardens and landscaped areas. The critics were already noting that the system was over sophisticated and had little prospect of remaining operational beyond a year given the absence of local skills to keep it working correctly.

The tower stood on a concrete plinth, providing a new and prominent landmark in the surrounding flat plains. It carried a large sign mounted on the large header tank, proudly proclaiming the name of the estate 'Muldoon', in a striking font with a fancy logo showing a stylized Mining Gantry with a pyramid-shaped spoil mountain in the background. The steel access ladder for servicing the tower was an irresistible attraction for a mob of small boys, who assumed it had been provided specially for them as play sculpture. An irritable security guard stationed nearby was growing grumpier by the minute, having to haul them off for their own safety.

"I'll bet you most of the locals think it's an abomination," commented Raegan, noticing Sens interest in this magnificent edifice. But Sens found himself disagreeing with his cousin on this point, having held a longstanding interest in machinery and engineering. "I suppose I have an engineer's feeling about what they have produced here. Some might not think this is beautiful, but I cannot help admiring its purpose in reducing our greenhouse gas emissions," he said.

"Well I suppose it's good to be an idealist," said Raegan, patronizingly. "I'm just wondering how long it will last, and whether it can be kept secure from the local kids, for that matter. They roam round after dark without any supervision at all and think nothing of helping themselves to whatever's around and…"

"Dad!" interrupted Meg, "Just listen to yourself, will you? What sort of impression do you think you're giving our guest?"

Sens could not help warming to his new-found relative and the way she had embraced him into her family. "It's okay," he said with a smile. "I'm under no illusions about how things are in this area. There are bad kids everywhere and it's usually because they haven't got enough to do. I think that the best we could do would be to give them responsibility for a place like this—looking after the gardens and making sure they're watered; keeping the turbines and machinery lubricated or whatever maintenance it needs—those sorts of activities."

"In your dreams," said Raegan.

"Dad…" said Meg again in a warning voice.

"A lot of things like that have been tried in the past," continued Raegan. "They lasted five minutes."

"We've just got to keep trying," Meg protested.

At that point any further discussion on the tricky question of managing problem children was drowned out by an announcement over the PA that the Senator JC Williams had kindly agreed to open the Muldoon Estate.

Williams, dressed for the occasion with a check shirt, beige cotton trousers and shiny brown boots, manufactured by the company founded by an unrelated namesake, RM Williams, had been standing to one side of the rostrum, talking quietly to one of his minders. The overall impact of his carefully selected dress was marred by a bulging beer gut, tethered in by an impressive looking leather belt and shiny gold buckle. His faux country look drew even more attention as he moved center stage, in front of the microphone. Here quite a crowd had gathered, blissfully unaware of the concern that would have generated in Sydney where the virulent pandemic was raging and the need for social distancing rigidly policed.

Large sweat stains had appeared under his armpits as he flayed the air ineffectually, trying to deter a myriad bush flies with one hand while holding a crumpled piece of paper with his notes in the other.

"My fellow Australians," he started, as though he were addressing an election audience, "I must first acknowledge with respect the traditional owners of the land on which we stand, the Ngiyampaa, Murawariand,

and Yuwalaraay peoples and their immense legacy to this place."

William's speech, on advice from his minders and his long-suffering ghost-writer, had clearly targeted the fact that the majority of the audience were young families with children. After his opening, he began with a story of his own background "as an ordinary son of a country family" who had to make his way in the world via the sacrifice of his parents and his own enterprise and "belief in the rights of the underdog."

He said that he had joined the Australian Grazers' Party, aware of the huge contribution that former luminaries such as Joh Bjelke Petersen and Robert Menzies had made in improving rural prosperity. He finished his shameless politicking by calling to arms his audience for the next election: "And we should remind ourselves that were it not for the Grazers', who have enabled development projects like this, we'd be enjoying a collapsed economy, as has occurred under successive Labor Administrations. People like myself, born and bred in a rural environment, can be relied on to ensure that the welfare of country people remains foremost in the minds of all governments in this great nation of ours."

"It therefore gives me great pleasure…"

Williams had stopped mid-sentence when he realized he had lost his audience; they had been distracted by the curious behaviour of a pack of dogs. The dogs had suddenly appeared from around the estate and had begun walking slowly around the base of the power tower in single file.

While Williams had been giving his speech, Sens had neglected to keep Marshall beside him, and his dog had wandered off to make friends with a motley assortment of other dogs beside the barbeque, watching for tidbits from the cook or the consumers of chops and sausages that were being handed out to all and sundry.

Marshall somehow 'took charge of the pack' (as was commented on subsequently by many of the sausage eaters) so that they began to follow him. The line of dogs walked with military-like precision and discipline, without barking or heel-nipping. He led them to the power tower and sat supervising as they walked around the base of the tower in a circle.

Williams was still at the lectern watching the curious spectacle of the dogs surrounding him. Then he noticed that the people behind the dogs had shifted their attention to the sky. One or two people stared excitedly, pointing out something to each other. Williams followed their gaze and could now see a black cigar-shaped craft large enough to blot out the sun. It made no sound and had suddenly appeared from nowhere. Sounds of excitement were taken over by shouts of alarm and people began to back away as the tower, and everything surrounding it for quite a distance, became enveloped in an impenetrable mist.

The dogs began howling in chorus as the mist was briefly illuminated by a brilliant cone of light from the craft, which was hovering (as some witnesses estimated) above a thousand meters. The howling of the dogs stopped abruptly and the light vanished. The mist slowly dissipated revealing that the entire pack of dogs had gone, excluding Marshall, who had wandered back to Sens and was sitting quietly beside him. The rostrum was also empty as the Senator and his minder had disappeared as well. The frantic searching for the rest of the afternoon proved fruitless as no one was able to find any trace of them whatsoever.

CHAPTER 13 Refuge and revelation

Once the hubbub had died slightly, Sens, Raegan and Meg headed straight for Raegan's ATV. They could hear the wailing of a siren in the distance and see a dust plume approaching very fast along the dirt road that accessed Muldoon. They joined a queue of other vehicles trying to leave via the same route, panicked by the strange events they had witnessed.

The atmosphere as they headed off was tense, nobody wanting to volunteer their thoughts. Sens concentrated on the road ahead and Marshall lay in the back of the ATV, panting softly as though nothing had happened.

As they drove onto the main road and accelerated in the direction of Cobar, Raegan finally broke the silence.

"I don't like what's going on here with that dog of yours, Sens. We all watched him rounding up those dogs like he was in a circus. What happened to those dogs? How come they all disappeared along with Senator Williams? Does he have something to do with the UFO? What's going on!" He looked really confused and was clearly wondering whether Sens was responsible for Marshall's antics. Meg stared out of the window, saying nothing. Sens appeared to be at a loss to know what he should say. He just shrugged his shoulders.

"The truth is I do not understand it either," Sens finally said in a low voice.

"He's your dog—I find this hard to believe?"

"Dad, please don't make an issue of this. I think Uncle Sens is dealing with things the best he can, and I'm quite sure that what happened to Senator Williams was completely unexpected."

"Yes, that is the truth. Whatever was responsible for Williams and his minder disappearing also caused Marshall's strange behaviour. That's all I can tell you," Sens said.

It was fortunate for everyone that they had left the scene so quickly, because no sooner had Sens finished his explanation, than they heard the sound of another police ATV. It swept past dangerously close leaving a thick cloud of dust in its wake.

"You'd better get moving, Dad," urged Meg. "I don't think talking to the police at this moment is a very good idea."

Without saying anything further, Raegan put his foot down. The stillness on their drive home felt like a thunderstorm about to break.

« »

Sens was furious with the Nest for their involvement in the Muldoon abduction since it involved his dog and, by extension, him. The moment he had an opportunity to challenge him in the privacy of the backyard of Raegan's home, he tried to contact the Nest. He simply focused his questions while thinking about the voice that had first come into his head. The response was immediate.

Can you explain to me precisely what your network is up to? Why are you abducting people and animals?

We have our reasons.

That's not good enough—unless you give me a plausible explanation, I am going to talk to the authorities about you.

Do you think they would believe you?

Given what you have been up to lately, maybe they would.

Our Nest does not think it likely—in fact, we have calculated a probability of close to 100% certainty that no one in authority will listen to what sound like crazy delusions.

Sens was not interested in hiding the intense frustration and anger he was feeling. *I want you to vacate Marshall immediately and leave us in peace!*

I'm afraid that we cannot agree to that.

You give me no choice then. Rather than allowing this to continue, I may be forced to act.

We don't like threats, particularly empty ones.

Why have you abducted Williams and a pack of innocent dogs? I want an explanation immediately.

There was a long pause as though the Nest was computing an appropriate response to this new ultimatum.

Sens, the voice had taken on a warm conciliatory tone, *we understand that your outburst is triggered by an emotional response rather than a logical or intelligent appreciation of our status. We have therefore decided to give you some sound advice, so listen carefully before doing something which you would live to regret.*

Firstly, we should explain that our Nest is engaged in experimentation with certain of your animal species, including dogs, aimed at understanding biological connections with your current pandemic disease. The person you know as Senator Williams has been required for complex reasons which we are not prepared to disclose at this time.

Secondly, we give you an undertaking that all animals which are subject to our experimentation will be returned to your planet, unharmed and unaware of what has taken place, at the conclusion of our experiments.

Thirdly, we can assure you that what we are doing is in the best interests of both your planet and your people, who face a catastrophe that will affect many millions more if allowed to proceed un-checked.

Fourthly, we strongly advise you not to try taking 'action', as you call it, because that will almost inevitably damage both Marshall and yourself, both physically and emotionally, and it will not prevent the implementation of our plan, nor delay it. We have reserve hosts available if necessary.

Finally, we must remind you of the immense superiority of our knowledge and technology compared to your own. To resist our plans would be completely futile. So we ask you to contemplate the only two choices that you have available. You can continue to cooperate with us, which as we have told you is in your planet's best interests, or you can attempt to obstruct our plans, which we cannot allow to happen and will only result in unimaginable grief for you if you try. We leave you to think about this.

Sens' further attempts to discuss the situation he was in met with complete silence, leaving him with feelings of helplessness and frustration. It was increasingly obvious that the Nest were acting in their own best interests, treating him and Marshall as pawns in their grand plans for the planet.

« »

While Sens was deciding whether he could act in some way, and with Marshall fast asleep in the garage, Meg quietly suggested to him that they should get some air and have a chat. As soon as they were by themselves, she said conspiratorially: "Some of the things I'm going to tell you even Dad doesn't know about, and I would like it to stay that way." Sens intrigued nodded in agreement.

"See, I belong to a group. We call ourselves the Cobarbarians; we just want the public to see us as bikies. Like we're the road warriors around here, come rain, wind or shine, Brmmmm!" She pointed at her shiny bike parked in garage. Sens couldn't help chuckling at her subversive sketch. But then her expression became serious again.

"In reality our group has an undercover purpose, to unseat the rednecks at every opportunity, the likes of Senator John Williams…"

Sens put up his hand, feeling a little uncomfortable that he should be learning stuff about Meg's life that she'd been keeping from her father. "Why are you telling me this?" he asked.

"Mainly because of what's just happened at Muldoon. I think maybe we're in the same boat, or at least that's what the authorities might think. Dad's obviously worried about what he saw and so am I."

Rodney Jensen

"Why don't you tell me your story first," said Sens.

"Okay," said Meg. "The fact is that the Cobarbarians have attracted the attention of the police already. We've had several run-ins and a prosecution recorded against one of our members..." she said, hesitating at this point.

"Anything else?" prompted Sens.

"Yes, I'm responsible for uncovering some pretty damaging stuff about Williams which has been published in the *Nyngan Examiner*. The information I provided is accurate, and I can prove it - I've done the research and know first-hand about some of it. But it could look bad for me from the police's point of view."

"What type of information," asked Sens.

"The research I did showed that Williams' own property development company was involved in the construction of the Muldoon Estate. There was a clear conflict of interest which of course he never declared."

"I'm starting to see where you're going with this," said Sens. "You think that the police are going to connect you with the Williams abduction—perhaps as a result of an elaborate hoax by your undercover organization, right?"

"Yes, I'm worried that's exactly what it could look like—but I am as much in the dark about what actually happened as you say you are. Though what puzzles me is that you seemed extremely evasive when Dad was asking you questions about Marshall. You've got something to hide, don't you? I think you do."

Meg's direct question put Sens on the back foot. How much should he trust her with his incredible story, which could impact both of them? Would she really believe that he'd been receiving messages from extraterrestrials via Marshall, or would she think he was a nutter?

Since his last conversation with the Nest, things had taken on an entirely new perspective, some inkling of their real motives becoming more obvious. He mulled it over and then decided that he must confide in her. She seemed to like him and appeared sympathetic, but would she hear him without dismissing what had to say as beyond belief?

"OK, I should probably start with Marshall. You've heard of possession?"

"Yesss…" Meg replied, frowning at something that already seemed to make her uncomfortable. "You telling me your dog's possessed?"

"There's more to it than that."

"Try me."

"OK, here goes: Marshall has been channeling messages to me from an extra-terrestrial network."

"Sorry, I am not up with that jargon! What does that mean?"

"It's a type of artificial intelligence network like we have here on earth, except that it is intelligence way beyond anything we on Earth are capable of and it comes from out there, not from any agency down here. And I carry on conversations with them in my head."

Rodney Jensen

"You mean it's from somewhere out in space and you hear strange voices in your head?" Meg asked incredulously.

Sens nodded solemnly. "I didn't believe it myself at first, but there have been things which Marshall has done that can't be explained any other way. The voice isn't at all like a dog might communicate, I can promise you! And Marshall, since he became possessed, has been able to do things that no normal dog can do. Rounding up those dogs at the Muldoon opening, for example. But there have been others."

"You've got to be kidding me, haven't you?" Meg was looking like she thought Sens had gone mad.

"I wish it were a joke, but it isn't. When this network first contacted me via Marshall, I thought that I was in a bad dream. Then an inexplicable thing happened involving a pet store and puppies disappearing and I realized this was not simply a nightmare. It was real. But it has its plusses. On the way out here fairly close to Bourke, Marshall's possession saved my life. I had caught a tick and he called an ambulance to pick me up from the roadside. I wouldn't be here otherwise. The incident is on police and hospital records, if you don't believe me."

"I really don't know what to believe. You telling me that you're the only one hearing these voices?"

Sens nodded. "That's right. It's all in my head. Nobody else can hear them. But suddenly they have started doing things that are more obvious to other people and I have no control over what's going on. Now

I'm being blamed for what Marshall's been doing, and I have to admit I am scared."

Sens paused to drag a tissue out of his pocket and blow his nose. He could no longer look Meg in the eye, afraid of what she must be thinking.

"Like Senator Williams and those dogs Marshall rounded up?" she mused.

"That's right."

Meg paced around the garden, pondering what Sens had been saying for a few moments. He sat down on a wooden bench waiting patiently to hear what she might suggest. Finally, she turned and sat down beside him. She took his hand and looked at him with a soft expression of sympathy. Sens suddenly felt a connection and affection that had not been there before. He returned her gaze calmly, waiting to hear what she would say.

"Supposing I'm the police, and I've been interviewing all those people who were watching what happened. What do you think they would make of it? That somebody around here was out to get Williams. Whoever that was, rigged up an elaborate hoax using trained dogs, a trapdoor under the stage, mist machine and a radio-controlled drone. Otherwise, they'd be struggling to find rational explanations for what can't be explained." Meg continued.

"Maybe there's someone around here that's into filmmaking or plays, someone that's got a serious grudge against Williams?" She mused.

"Yes, that would certainly be a more acceptable explanation as far as the police are concerned than an extraterrestrial explanation, and takes the pressure off Marshall and me. But given what you've now just told me, I'm worried that you're squarely in the frame with your article damming Williams. You'd have to expect that the police are fully aware of what the Cobarbarians are up to, wouldn't you?"

"You're right. Whichever way those events are interpreted one of us is in deep shit."

"I'm so sorry that Marshall and I have created this problem. It's way beyond me to fix it now." said Sens.

He'd become broken, visibly shrunken and aged ten years in the past few minutes. Confiding in Meg was forcing him to confront his worst fears.

"What's going to happen to Marshall? There are people in government who will already know what took place at the Muldoon Estate. They'll want to take him away and do horrible experiments on his brain or whatever. I'd prefer to have him put down than allow that to happen," he said, dabbing his cheeks with his handkerchief.

Meg put a comforting arm around his shoulder. "Don't panic, we'll think of something. But first of all, this is what we must do. We've got to pack our things and get out of here immediately."

"What will Reagan think?"

"I'm not sure, but probably relieved to see the back of us right now. I never talk to him about my stuff with the

Cobarbarians, but I am sure he can sense there is an underlying agenda with the club. It's definitely time for us to get out of here for all our sakes. Just be positive is my advice."

CHAPTER 14 Sam and Byron investigate Muldoon Abductions

Two days before their period of quarantine was to end, Sam and Byron received an urgent call from Graves. "There's been another sighting and incident which seems to indicate that the extra-terrestrials have lifted the stakes by abducting a prominent politician. Please arrange to visit the site immediately. I'm attaching a copy of the police report."

« »

The sun was high in a cloudless sky. A pair of Galahs were perched on Muldoon's services tower ignoring the world beneath. Kids of all ages were everywhere—kicking balls, skate-boarding along half-finished pathways and jumping their board fearlessly off ramps they'd built from surplus bricks and scrap timber. The whole development had a half-completed, work-suspended look about it.

"Do you think this place is ever going to be finished properly?" remarked Byron.

"It's the weekend remember! We've been in quarantine too long." Sam reminded him. "Ah! There's our contact."

A tall man in a wide brimmed hat was standing by himself and staring at the children's antics. He held out a hand as he saw them approaching. "Jim Neverglade," he introduced himself, "the Senator's minder's assistant."

"Thanks for meeting us. It must still come as a shock to recalling what happened. Are you able to talk about it now? It really helps us to interview an eye-witness," said Sam.

Jim wanted to know more about them but Sam fended of his questions calling themselves 'special investigators for the police'. She was wary of putting any idea of extra-terrestrial involvement into the man's head if he had any other explanation.

"To tell you the truth, I'm still coming to terms with whatever happened to John and Adam."

"Adam?" Byron asked

"Adam was Senator William's minder or 'events manager' to give him his proper title? I helped Adam in the office..."

"Let's go back to the start of what you can recall," Sam interrupted. "Firstly can you show us exactly where John and Adam were standing when the incident happened?"

"Yes that's easy. We'd asked the contractors to put down a few pavers where we could set up a rostrum and a table for the P/A system. The pavers are still where they were, they're quite close to the Services Tower as you can see," he said pointing at a square patch of paving. "I think William's speech was going to refer to it as an important contributor to sustainability or some such bullshit!"

He led them to the paved area. "So the rostrum was about here and the audience was standing around the paved area. Williams was facing towards the tower and the audience was mostly between him and the tower."

"In the report we've read there was reference to a pack of dogs. Where were they?" Byron asked.

"To tell you the truth, I was standing next to the P/A system and didn't really notice the dogs until they started howling together. It was a horrible noise and nearly all in the audience were turning to get a look at what was going on. But I still couldn't see the dogs because there were too many people in the way."

"Can you tell us what happened next?" asked Sam.

"While the dogs were howling, the sky suddenly became dark and then we were surrounded in a mist. It was a thick one like we sometimes get around here in mid-winter. Some of the people were pointing up at the sky, and I searched to see what they were excited about. Then I saw a very faint outline of what looked like one of those zeppelins the Germans used before planes were invented. Then, next thing I knew, the dogs had stopped howling. I turned to ask Adam who'd been standing quite close to where I was what the hell was going on and he'd gone. Then I noticed that there was no one standing at the rostrum either. Williams was gone too! It could've been me..." Jim was having trouble continuing.

"Take your time," said Sam and put a comforting arm over his shoulder. "It's important that we know everything that happened, even if what you witnessed is something you have never experienced before and find hard to believe."

"That is all I can really remember. At first I thought the Senator and Adam must have wandered off when the mist came down. But later once I discovered that all the dogs had disappeared as well, I had to accept that perhaps I was never going to see either of them again. It's a nightmare. It could have been me. I can't stop thinking about it." He pulled a large handkerchief out of his pocket and blew noisily into it.

Sam looked questioningly at Byron who'd been recording their interview, wondering whether he had anything more to ask. He shook his head.

"Jim, I have just one final question to ask you?" Sam had waited patiently for him to recover himself. "Can you think of anyone or any organization that could have staged a very elaborate hoax to abduct the Senator under the cover of the mist?"

Jim thought for several seconds. "I have racked my brains but if they had been taken by anyone under my nose they'd have had to be drugged first and that clearly wasn't so."

Sam tapped Jim's holo with her contact details and let him go.

Byron quietly said to Sam. "The report mentioned that this entire area has been checked for any such possibility including hidden trapdoors and underground passageways. They found nothing like that."

"I know, of course. I've read the report. I was more interested to discover whether he knew more about William's involvement in Final Solution."

Rodney Jensen

« »

After Sam and Byron were released from Quarantine they were thoroughly de-briefed by Graves. Grave's two principal concerns were the risk of an expanding pandemic making UFODD no longer secure, and secondly, the recent increase in sightings and abductions.

Sam explained to Graves, "I am just going to recapitulate some relevant reports Byron and I have filed. In addition to our investigations in Queensland, the thing that stands out is the connection with a man we interviewed in Wirrabera, a retired Qantas pilot Sens Petersen and his sheepdog called 'Marshall'. We interviewed Petersen shortly after he and his dog were implicated in a theft of puppies at the same time as a UFO was seen hovering over the town. A short time after that, Petersen's house burnt to the ground in suspicious circumstances. Petersen and his dog then disappeared. The next thing we discovered was the dog had been temporarily staying on a property near Bourke where he exhibited capabilities far beyond that of any normal sheepdog. Petersen at the time was temporarily separated from his dog while staying in hospital suffering from tick bite. On regaining consciousness it was reported by his doctor that he was sure it was his dog who'd called the ambulance. The matter was referred to an external psychologist who came to the conclusion that the man was delusional but presented no risk to the public and could be discharged."

"As you know, Byron and I followed up the recent incident at the Muldoon Opening. Our contact had no explanation for what occurred. But we subsequently found that one of the people interviewed by the police after the event was able to identify both Petersen and his dog from photographs they were shown. Several other witness reports provided by the police noted that Petersen's dog had seemed to be doing very strange things rounding up other dogs on the estate while the opening address took place.

"Finally we have a new suspect, one Meg Oswald, who was identified at the Muldoon Opening together with Petersen. She is reported to have been involved in political activities against the Senator, but whether or not that is coincidental with his abduction we have no evidence as yet. Our problem is that at the moment we have no idea of the whereabouts of Petersen, Oswald, or the dog. The police have contacted Oswald's father in Cobar, but he claims to have no idea where they are right now either. In short, they seem to have done a runner, which in itself adds to our suspicion that they have something to hide."

Graves thought for a moment. "I suppose they could be anywhere by now including Queensland, South Australia and Victoria. Please coordinate with Bourke Command and request the police set up road blocks at all the main roads leading interstate. At this stage let's tell the police that we suspect they are pandemic carriers. Also have them to circulate photographs of Petersen and Oswald to other police stations. It's a long shot but they've got to come to ground some time."

CHAPTER 15 Behind the media

Following Sam and Byron's debriefing, UFODD arranged a meeting with Bourke Police Command officers who were in charge of inquiries into the abortive Muldoon opening.

Sam had discussed with Commander Graves how she wanted the meeting to be structured. He told her that it was imperative to remain guarded in what she divulged, as from his own experience there was automatic disbelief in government offices the moment extra-terrestrial sightings were mentioned. Similarly, he referred to UFODD's strict secrecy protocols, meaning that any subject matter to be discussed must have been already cleared by his own staff.

The meeting was held via a secure holo-link with Special Agents Mitchell and Lowe facing Commander Matthew Preston and DCI Peter Burn in the Bourke Police offices.

"Thank you for agreeing to meet us," she said politely. "I'm calling in my official position as a Special Agent for the Unidentified Flying Object and Defense Directorate from our regional offices near Bourke."

"Yes, we are aware of your location," said Preston. "UFODD lies within our patch, but I'm intrigued because this is actually the first time anyone from your organization has ever called us."

"Generally, we prefer to keep a low profile; there is often public disquiet about the subject of our investigations. But I'm contacting you in relation to the recent incident at the Muldoon Group Housing opening which has definitely raised the bar a notch."

"Meaning what exactly?"

"As you are probably aware, we investigate any incidents which may relate to UFO contacts. The number of contacts we have recorded in the past few weeks is unprecedented. Most of these have been in the form of abductions of dogs and bats. But the Muldoon contact involved a human abduction and, as far as I'm aware, that is unprecedented."

"Senator John Williams?"

"Correct, Commander. And we have two main requests concerning this matter. The first is that this and any further discussions we have remain confidential between our respective organizations. The second is that if any new information comes to light about this or related inquiries, that you will refer them to us immediately."

"Naturally, details of our conversations will remain confidential but I am not sure about your second request. It will depend on the nature of the information we uncover. I will not commit to passing over to you any information which for whatever reason we consider should remain for our eyes only," said Preston.

Before responding, Sam nudged Byron who seemed agitated and about to say something. Their eyes met and she shook her head slightly to make sure he kept quiet.

"Thank you for being open about this, Commander Preston. But I need to refer you to the Commonwealth memorandum of understanding with UFODD, originally signed and sealed in December 2029 in Canberra. You may be unfamiliar with the details of this important agreement. It covers the protocol of communications between UFODD and State Authorities including police forces in Australia. My assistant Byron Lowe here can send you a copy if you wish?"

"OK, if you wouldn't mind sending us the document and depending on what it says and my judgment of what is or what is not appropriate to give you, we will do our best to comply with your wishes. But in return for our cooperation, I would like you to brief me and my Case Officer DCI Burn. Perhaps DCI Burn and your Agent Lowe can liaise on a regular basis."

"Yes, I am happy to have Byron do that, and thank you for your assistance in this matter."

With that, Sam excused herself and left Byron to explain more about their mission. She could tell that he was pleased that she was trusting him at last to take on such an important role.

Three days after the event, Byron and Sam were at their desks poring through the data they had collated on their various sightings. They were still trying to track down Meg, Sens, and his remarkable sheepdog. Their efforts had drawn a blank on their immediate whereabouts, when an unexpected holo-comm came through. Sam took the call.

"Yes, that's me," she said, her brow furrowing as she listened more intently. "Yes, we've all seen the article." Byron, who had only been half listening to the interchange, stopped what he was doing and gestured to Sam to switch over to speaker mode so he could listen in properly.

« »

Sam's initial contact with the editor of the *Nyngan Examiner* had not been promising. His tone was impatient and uncompromising: "There's no point discussing this further. I do not know who Stephen Kay's contact was and I'd never ask him anyway. You should realize that this publication has a proud tradition of keeping sources confidential. We think they should be given the same respect as a church confession," he said. The man was obviously on a roll and warming to a familiar rant.

"But," he went on, "we're fully aware that the courts are happy to trample over our wishes and ignore the rights of our sources. Be that as it may—it's usually a matter of poor judgment by the prosecutors, or the legal geniuses having a total disregard for the realities of journalism. If we didn't have this policy nobody would ever tell us anything, and the public would be kept in the dark just like the Communist regimes operate." Finally, in a more conciliatory tone, he added: "However, what I can offer you is that I could request the source to come forward, under conditions of anonymity and protection from any further investigation or action."

Sam had politely declined that offer, which in any case she had no authority to accept. So when she received a call from the very man they wanted to talk to, the author of the report on Senator Williams, she didn't delay. She looked up her schedule and checked with Byron, who nodded his assent. "Just give us an hour and we'll be right over," she said.

The two Agents arrived early, using UFODD's ATV. They'd had time to discuss how they should approach the interview, given the unhelpful reception they had initially received from the *Nyngan Examiner's* editor. They agreed beforehand that they should be careful not to divulge any information on which Stephen Kay might be tempted to base a feature article. They both suspected that he would be viewing the meeting as a 'fishing expedition', but they were to be surprised.

The offices of the *Nyngan Examiner* were centrally located close to where the former railway station had been. The buildings were old and had a railway look about them. The two Agents entered via an uncared-for frontage and an open doorway, flanked by small, barred windows. They walked down a dingy corridor into the engine room of the *Nyngan Examiner.* It was a largish area containing a clutter of rusted metal furniture and papers haphazardly stored on every spare surface. It seemed like a quaint reminder of the 20th century, with no obvious effort to achieve paperless systems, despite the leap in technologies relegating paper to the archives in most capital city offices. There were three workstations in the room, but only one of them was occupied. Sam could hardly resist smiling at the age of the computer line-up they were using. She would not have been surprised to see a Windows-based system still hiding away in a cupboard somewhere.

A gaunt looking man, crouched over his comms unit, got up to greet them. He moved with a slight limp and needed a walking stick to get around. He had a permanently intense expression, accentuating the lines across his forehead and cheeks, and his conversation was punctuated with a nervous twitch at the corners of his mouth.

"Stephen Kay," he introduced himself, extending his hand. "Meteor said that you wanted to talk to me?"

"Actually he made it pretty clear that YOU didn't," Byron batted the ball back at him.

Sam looked at her partner, with an expression warning him to shut up. She'd been thinking lately that his lack of diplomacy had been improving, but he still seemed to revert to his habit of turning everything into a joke, and he had a strange knack of putting her fellow countrymen offside with brash remarks supposed to be clever. However, Stephen took Byron's remark seriously, scratched his neck and fiddled with his pencil before continuing.

"There's some background on the Muldoon story, which I think you should know," he said at last. Sam held up her hand to stop him from going on.

"Your editor made it pretty clear that you have consistently protected your sources. I'm sure I don't have to remind you that anything you tell me from now on has to go on the record, whether or not that endangers your source. I want you to be clear you've thought through the implications of what you're about to tell us, although we're convinced that there is a strong public interest justification for you to do so."

"I appreciate you saying that, and I do know what I'm doing; I really want to try to help someone avoid a miscarriage of justice," he said.

"Okay," said Sam pulling out her holo. "We're recording this. What was it you wanted to tell us?"

"In my story about Senator Williams, there was a lot more I could have said. In particular there is something that happened a long time ago and involved both him and Meg Oswald and might help you to understand a lot more about what's going on."

"Meg Oswald? I don't think there was any reference to her in your article."

"No that's right. She is the adopted daughter of a Cobar family I've known a long time. But the fact is, her life intersected with Williams quite some time ago."

"It so happens that Meg Oswald is a person of interest to us, for reasons which are also confidential. So remember what we've said. If you're about to implicate Meg as your source for the piece, she could possibly end up in trouble," Byron said quietly.

"Given the fact that you already appear to have her on your radar, what I'm about to tell you might cause you to rethink what you're doing," said Stephen. "It all happened a long time ago, on the weekend of a 'Bachelors and Spinsters Ball'."

In a quiet aside to Byron, Sam explained: "It's a tradition for country towns here to hold formal events like these. They help young people living on isolated properties get together."

"I can't remember the exact date," Stephen resumed, "But Meg had just graduated from college and met this guy Damien Hartley who was working as a biologist in Nyngan at the time. Sometime later they'd been at the ball and it seemed like they were becoming really attached. They were driving back to her place after the ball, it was late at night and Damien was at the wheel." Stephen paused to take a sip of water from a bottle on his desk before continuing.

"Damien was a really smart guy—not much older than Meg but obviously working on important stuff, which he only talked about in the vaguest of terms. He usually worked at a special research place—nobody could go near it without a pass. I suspected that he must be working on contract for a pharmaceutical company or something like that."

"Is that all you can tell us about him?" asked Sam.

"In the times I met him it was clear that he was very dedicated, strong on all the environmental issues; he was concerned about our current global warming situation and the number of species we have already lost through human competition and mismanagement of habitat."

"But what about his actual work?" Sam pressed him impatiently.

"I've no idea. He would never talk about it and made it clear that whatever he was doing was classified, but clearly of great importance."

"So Meg had a really smart boyfriend who was clearly working on something quite important?" said Byron, wondering when the hesitant Stephen would get to the point.

"Yes, there is more to it but I'll come to it later," said Stephen, his twitch returning. "Anyway, back to the crash, it was a dark night and as they were driving along, they came to a bend in the road. Just at this point this idiot driving an ATV with his spotlights on high beam came careering round the corner on the wrong side of the road, right into their path. Damien swerved to avoid a collision and got onto the loose gravel on the shoulder. His vehicle rolled and burst into flames. Meg was able to get out and so was the passenger in the front, though injured, but Damien didn't make it."

"You mean he died on the scene?" Byron asked.

"Yes, there was nothing that could be done." His voice had become choked up and he had to pause for a moment to compose himself. "But the four wheel drive that caused all the accident didn't stop," he finally managed to get out.

"So what happened then?" asked Sam.

"Meg had a mobile phone with her, and an ambulance eventually turned up…I suppose."

"What do you mean 'you suppose,' you were there weren't you?" Sam demanded, losing patience with his attempt to cover up his obvious involvement in the incident.

Stephen looked like a frightened animal caught in a spotlight. He slowly nodded.

"What a dick! Do you seriously think you could have withheld that vital piece of information from us?" Byron remarked. Sam shot him a glance that said *calm down!*

"I suppose not..." Stephen finally muttered, before continuing. "There was an inquest, of course, and the police had pretty strong evidence that the ATV that caused this accident was driven by John Williams, son of a wealthy grazier in this locality. John's dad had a great deal of clout, not only with the local police but also with the judiciary. It's like that in a small place like this. But it's not good for criminal justice," Stephen said bitterly.

"Do you have a record of the inquest?" asked Sam.

"Yes, I do. If I can find it, I will send you a copy," said Stephen.

"The evidence against Williams was basically circumstantial, but pretty damning all the same. On that same evening and not very far from the scene of the accident, he was pulled over by the police for driving fast and erratically. But he had no blood alcohol reading according to their evidence. Not only that, but the forensic team subsequently worked out that at the speed the ATV had been driving when he was pulled over, there was a very strong probability that it was his vehicle which had caused the accident. The time on Damien's broken watch correlated very closely to the time and distance it took the ATV to be pulled over by the police at the estimated speed it had been travelling."

Stephen paused a moment to make sure they understood what he was telling them.

"You mean the vehicle that was presumed to have caused the accident?" Sam asked.

"That's right," said Stephen. "It was quite late, and there were no other cars on that lonely stretch of road at that time of night. The police, when they stopped William's ATV, had seen no other vehicles for at least half an hour, and the ATV fitted the description exactly of a four-wheel drive with powerful spotlights mounted on a 'roo bar."

"There are multiple four-wheel drives in this locality that have 'roo bars and spotlights. That's hardly unusual is it?" Sam remarked.

"Yes, as I said the evidence was circumstantial. But to make sure his son got off the charge, William's influential father flew in the most eminent barrister he could find from the big end of town in Sydney. The barrister did as was expected of him and made mincemeat of the police's evidence. Williams himself kept his head, never admitting his guilt. In any event, he effectively got off with a six-month suspension of his license and a $500 fine. Meg lost the man of her life and the person she thought responsible got off scot-free."

Stephen took another swig from his water bottle and blew his nose with a grimy handkerchief.

"What more can you tell us about Williams when he was younger?" asked Sam.

"I don't know much about him. He went to a private school and had an MBA by the time this all happened. He seemed to be something of a hot-shot with his market manipulation, and the way he worked his farm was far more unusual than the practices most farmers followed around here.

"What do you mean?"

"I don't have the details, but he was a pioneer in the use of drought resistant crops, he used technology like drones to monitor things and he kept his eye on what would most likely be wanted in ten years' time, rather than tomorrow. He was also an efficient manager and preferred to have someone taking care of the day to day while he was off in Canberra for much of the time. He wasn't seen around here much except at election time."

"You don't like him do you? Is there something personal, more than the fact that you knew Meg?" asked Byron.

"What was there to like about him?"

"Now back to these property dealings which you've written about recently. Am I correct in what you're saying is that Meg was your source?" asked Sam.

"That's only partly correct. We worked on the story together, if you want to know."

"She obviously had good reason to hate the guy—but so did you. It looks like the accident caused permanent damage to you. Yet you haven't disclosed this in the very negative article you collaborated on have you?"

Stephen looked cagily back at her, the twitch at the corner of his mouth wildly out of control.

"I'll take that as a 'yes', shall I?" Sam said with finality.

"Wow," said Byron, "and your boss espouses such high journalistic principles. Don't tell me that objective reporting by this paper is one of them."

"It certainly undermines everything you've reported in your piece, wouldn't you say?" remarked Sam, for once agreeing with the tone of her partner's criticism. "Why should we, or the public for that matter, believe anything that you've written about Williams, knowing that it's based on revenge? I don't suppose the Press Council would be too impressed either, given the damage to William's reputation."

"He can rot in hell as far as I care!" spat out Stephen. A gob of saliva was working its way down his chin, he'd become so worked up. "You come in here wet behind the ears and so fucking self-righteous. How dare you accuse me of biased reporting? You want to see the stuff on what we have based the article. It's all here!" He fumbled through some papers on his desk and almost threw a bundle at Byron. "Just take a look at that!"

Byron ignored the bundle of papers, which had fallen onto the floor. "So, what you're expecting us to believe is that all this research you've been uncovering is factually correct, despite your lack of objectivity?"

"The facts speak for themselves," said Stephen. "That man has made millions of dollars from the construction of the Muldoon Estate. The so called 'tender' was awarded to the construction company on a plate. Those papers prove that Williams is one of the so-called 'consultants' of that company. It was a small piece of information he neglected to tell the procurement people in the Commonwealth public service when he used his influence to ensure that they got the job. I hope it does finish his career in politics."

"I'm not sure what part Meg played in all this. How did you and she come by that information?" asked Sam.

"No comment," said Stephen.

"Be that as it may, she's still at large and we need to talk to her about what happened at Muldoon last weekend. Do you know where she is now?" she asked.

Stephen shied away from the question, getting up and walking to the window.

"I don't have any idea where she is," he said finally.

"But knowing how much Meg has already done to smear Senator Williams, it seems highly likely that she had something to do with his disappearance at the Muldoon Opening, wouldn't you say?"

Stephen paused, staring out of the window, before continuing. "Look, I wasn't there," he said finally, "but of course I have read some of the interviews and I wrote our lead story. I would be suggesting some possibility that this was an elaborate prank combining a drone and a ground-based smoke generator, something like that. I thought that was why you are so keen to get in touch with Meg, though I have absolutely no reason to suppose she was behind the abduction, other than the fact that I know why she detests the man so much."

Stephen wiped the sweat that was beading on his forehead, wrong footed and guilt written all over himself as it registered that he had inadvertently dropped his friend in it.

"Here's what we want," said Sam. Given that this woman is still at large, if you are in a position to contact her, I think you should pass on our request to get in touch with us urgently. You might stress that we act outside police jurisdiction. Our remit is far more than a matter of local crime. And this is not to appear in your publication unless you want to end up in court yourself."

Sam handed Kay a standard X-Notice. He looked carefully through it, noting that the powers laid down were draconian in the extreme. The words 'life imprisonment', 'solitary confinement' and 'high security correction facility' jumped off the page at him.

He nodded and silently escorted the two out of the building without saying another word.

« »

On the way back to base Sam and Byron shared their thoughts on the evasive and troubled Stephen Kay.

"He seemed to have no idea that Williams was in the employ of the Commonwealth Security and Intelligence Agency CSIA at the time of the accident," said Byron.

Sam had also formed a view of what Stephen was missing in his investigation. "He doesn't seem to have any inkling of what the Nyngan Lab was up to, let alone the fact that it was conducting germ warfare research at the behest of the US. It's now pretty obvious that was where this Damien person was working."

Byron nodded. "There can't be too many research labs in such a remote place. I think Kay's story about his Damien's death sounds more and more like conspiracy. We've both read the CSIA file on Williams, which supports his involvement in the accident. I don't think it's too big a leap for it to have been planned and deliberate, do you?"

Sam was still feeling her way with the implications of what they knew. "It looks that way, doesn't it? There must have been a reason if Williams planned to murder Damien in a car accident without realizing that other passengers would be involved. Maybe CSIA had come to the conclusion that Damien might be about to blow the whistle on the Nyngan research project. Maybe Williams got off with the light sentence because the magistrate was quietly pushed by CSIA, given the importance of the research from a national security perspective?"

"Is this speculation, or have you picked up on any other evidence to support your theory?" Byron asked.

"A bit of both. There is little doubt that Williams was the driver that caused the crash, although from what we've been told, he was never proven guilty despite the evidence pointing strongly at him. We need to check Damien Hartley's case-file to find out exactly why he was under security surveillance at the time. It would have had to be a serious security risk for Homeland to take such action. The possibilities are that either Williams took matters into his own hands or maybe someone higher up in CSIA decided to act and had him terminated with the help of a local agent."

"And that would have to have been Williams himself?" said Byron.

"I don't think that it would have been necessary to involve anyone else. And given the circumstances as Kay described them, it would have been quite easy for him to claim what happened was an accident while driving too fast. And as it happened, Williams didn't even get convicted of that. It's probably something that nobody will ever get to the bottom of. It's too cold a case," she said.

"Yes—I know pretty well the paranoia that existed in the US post 9/11 and what US Security were capable of there. They would have seen Damien as expendable and an unnecessary risk. It's clear that Williams has always been ambitious and would have leapt at this chance to ingratiate himself with the authorities."

"Except, I suspect that in reality he was just doing what he'd been told to do. That seems a lot more likely to me," Sam interjected. "He was probably working under orders from above, possibly the US.

"Anyway, Williams got what he wanted—became head of that facility. He may still be involved with their research, although the file indicates it was disbanded ten years ago," said Byron.

"And what about Meg? Do you think she worked any of this out? It would give her a stronger motive to collude in William's abduction given what he had done. Maybe Kay's idea wasn't all that fanciful," said Sam.

"Hang on, you're going too fast!" said Byron, "What about Final Solution? They would also have had a motive to dispose of Williams, assuming he was intending to out them?"

"I'm not sure," said Sam, "I suppose it's possible if they feared that Williams was going to risk his career despite the hold they had over him and bring it all out into the open. Perhaps he had a conscience after all. Perhaps he thought they would have developed the antidote for their own members' use," said Sam.

"Williams must have guessed that the information he gave Final Solution may have been responsible for the pandemic. I'd be betting he's been trying to track down whoever he was contacted by and expose them."

"I actually don't think Final Solution had anything to do with it. My training tells me that the abduction has all the hallmarks of extra-terrestrial work. It ties in with the other abductions in SE Queensland. The real mystery is what they're after. What is obvious is that we must find Meg and dig out of her what she knows."

"And I also wouldn't mind getting my hands on Sens, and that bloody mutt of his as well," said Byron.

PART 3

CHAPTER 16 Ulterior motives

From Reagan's home in Cobar, Sens, Meg and Marshall set off up the road to Louth. It was a straight and uneventful drive and they soon reached the center of the sleepy village that Louth, once a thriving town, had become. While Sens wasn't really in the mood for sightseeing, he couldn't resist briefly driving up the road towards Bourke. He then then turned back and tried the road leading to the Darling River bridge crossing a few kilometers to the north west. "I read that Louth was once famous for the invention of a piece of sheep shearing equipment, but its heyday was more than a century ago when the river served as the main transport artery of the inland."

"You been a schoolteacher or something?" Meg smiled.

"Nothing like that. Just something I read. The history of inland Australia fascinates me," he said.

He made a U-turn back to Louth and began heading south west, before pulling over to the side of the road. Meg had been following his erratic exploration around Louth on her MAP-XTRA App on her holo.

I think we should avoid Bourke for now, and we're not really equipped to take the lonely road across the river up to the Queensland border," said Meg, pointing at the aerial map for Sens' benefit. It showed the road they were on, was heading more or less parallel with the meandering track of the Darling River.

"Maybe we can find somewhere to camp beside the river further downstream?" She suggested. Sens already had that in mind, and they set off towards Wilcannia.

As they drove along the arrow straight road, the scenery remained semi-desert country. On their right, a belt of gum trees marked the edge of the river zone. The horizon lay ahead as far as the eye could see, with the ribbon of bitumen vanishing to a hazy point, eluding the naked eye. The sky above this empty landscape formed a huge dome of darkening blue, with fluffy highlights of white cloud. In the foreground the cloud layers were bathed in deepening shadow, while in the further distance, the color graded to lighter shades of salmon pink, reflecting the last rays of the setting sun to the west.

Somewhere between Louth and Tilpa, and guided by Sens' map, they turned down what soon became a very narrow dirt road heading directly towards a belt of trees, thickening to a sparse wood with spiky underbrush. Further along, the track wound its way gradually downwards, paralleling the turns of the river ahead. The sun had already set and the sky was quickly growing dark. They came to a low embankment beside the road and they could now see the track descending sharply along the face of a low cliff, with moonlight glimmering on a narrow stretch of water. The track went as far as the riverbank, then ran along it a further hundred meters or so. They continued along the track, coming to a wrecked hull, half-submerged in the river and permanently resting beside the bank. It had once been a paddle steamer, now left to gradually fall apart with gaping holes and rotted timbers in the superstructure.

Marshall without any inhibition took the lead and ran along a path to where a narrow hardwood plank connected the vessel's deck to the riverbank. He ran across and began sniffing up and down the deck, into cabins which had lost their doors and the captain's wheelhouse now an empty shell without a wheel.

Avoiding the spiders and mosquitoes, Meg and Sens carefully followed across the plank after making sure it was firmly bedded in place. Meg took one look at the state of the cabins and recoiled.

"I'm not going to spend the night here in case that's what you're thinking. It has a bad feeling about it. I'd prefer sleeping out under the stars than this. Let's get out of here!"

Sens *had* considered the possibility of using the cabin, but agreed with Meg. He wondered whether she might be sensing something more disturbing than a few spiders or snakes. He had also noticed that Marshall would not go into many of the derelict cabins, despite his normally inquisitive nature. He left his thoughts unspoken.

« »

In the spot where the steamer had ended its days, the river was only about forty meters wide. The track they had driven along was a narrow ledge between a cliff and the water. The red ochre cliff rose about ten meters, to the level of the surrounding plain. The opposite side of the river was also sheer cliff, leaving this section of river land to form a secluded canyon and a secure hidey-hole, unless by chance someone just happened to look down on them from the plain beyond the cliff. That was unlikely to happen unless they advertised their presence by lighting a fire or using bright lights at night. They would also immediately see or hear anyone coming in along the track, which came to an abrupt end just beyond them.

They returned to the ATV and looked at what they'd packed by way of camping gear. There was a tent, sleeping bags, water and a lantern. The rest of the space was taken up with cartons of food, a large plastic water container, a gas top and canister. Sens attended to Marshall's needs first, doling out dog biscuits and water into his bowls.

"That's all we've got. Sorry, Marshall!" said Sens. His dog sniffed at the biscuits and looked at him accusingly before crunching them down.

"I'll put up the tent; if you feel like cooking there are some tins of stuff which will do for now?" He said to Meg. She nodded seeing that Sens wanted to ask her something more. "There's only one airbed but it's big enough for both of us if that's ok?"

"I'll be safe in my sleeping bag. Don't you worry about that!" Meg smiled. "I'm looking forward to seeing you take a swim in the river tomorrow. I don't think the crocs come this far south, but you never know!" she hinted mischievously. "Come to think of it, we both probably need a wash."

Sens really wanted to say something clever, light-hearted and playful but contented himself with, "I think I'll be leaving my briefs on, thank you."

"Sorry, that's unacceptable. Modesty's not allowed around here. We're camping, remember." She was interrupted by Marshall, who had taken a swim in the river and come back to shake himself all over her, a token of his acceptance of her into doggyhood.

"Get off me, you wretch!" she shouted at him.

"He likes you," said Sens.

« »

Sens found it difficult to sleep that night with the changes in his friendship with Meg on his mind. He was suddenly experiencing feelings that he had long forgotten. There was something about her no-nonsense approach and casual familiarity that had broken through his barriers. She was making him feel more alive than he could remember.

Meg stirred, sensing that this strange, interesting man was not asleep.

"Do you want to talk more about your Intelligence Nest? I'm finding what you said difficult to take in," she started. "Do you think it has anything to do with the pandemic for example?"

"Not necessarily, there are many other explanations I'm aware of for pandemics. I remember from the COVID-19 pandemic one of the most prevalent theories was that animals kept in Chinese markets were responsible for the first outbreak, and is probably the most likely explanation for this present pandemic. The markets are still there, and I doubt whether they'll ever be eradicated. Could be the same with this pandemic?"

Meg yawned. "I've got to admit I've been following the stuff on the internet explaining the theories about how this pandemic started. Many people think it could have been a deliberate act, or maybe an experiment gone wrong by some bio lab that's been covered up."

"Conspiracy theory abounds on the internet, but in my book the accidental transmission from animal to human or a bio-experiment gone wrong are much more likely than any deliberate attempt to infect the planet."

"You probably haven't heard of Final Solution then. According to what I've read it's a growing theoretically Green but Ultra-Right Wing movement which sees the only way to stop global warming is by stopping it at source, i.e. getting rid of most humans—us not them, that is!"

"That sounds as dangerous as Nazi Germany!"

"Probably is, but I wasn't around then."

"Neither was I!" Sens remarked indignantly with a smile, "but I've read history. Hitler's motives weren't about protecting the planet from global warming. The 21st Century Final Solution followers are an even more sinister ultra-right-wing movement clothed in green camouflage."

Meg rolled over in her sleeping bag like a huge sausage, so that her face was much closer to Sens and the two could sense each other's bodies through their bedding. "Now don't get any ideas will you, but I just have an urge to whisper something in your ear," she said sleepily.

"I can tell you've got a kind heart because of that dog of yours, haven't you?"

"I suppose I do, I love Marshall, but I must admit at times people can drive me to distraction, and one thing I cannot abide is cruelty to animals."

"No, I don't like that much either." Meg paused wanting to know more about the real Sens without seeming crass.

"Ever been married, Sens?"

It was Sens' turn to feel exposed. "Yes, I was married for quite a long time, but in the end my wife and I went separate ways. I don't even think about her much these days. I don't even know if she's survived the pandemic."

"You don't miss her at all?"

"I suppose you could say we were good friends, but we were never very compatible for some reason. You could say I've become quite self-centered and I've been happy to live by myself with Marshall for quite a while now. But that's all changed. I don't have a place to go back to any longer. It all burnt down. And despite what the Nest assures me, I think they were behind it."

"Sens, why would you think they would do such a thing?"

Sens said nothing for a few moments. "Meg I'm not sure but for some obscure reason I think they wanted me to come out here and meet you."

"I'm not that important!" Meg laughed. "But it's nice that you should think that anyway. You're not serious, are you?"

"In all honesty, until just now I hadn't thought this through. But I've been thinking of what happened with Senator Williams and the dogs. Maybe that wouldn't have happened if I hadn't been there and maybe it wouldn't have happened without Marshall, or without you either. Do you get my drift?"

"Yes, but it seems a little…well, you know…"

"The ravings of a nutter?"

"Not that extreme, but a bit of a stretch I'd say."

« »

Sens and Meg decided that their camping spot was as good a place as any to remain hiding out for a few days. They had enough provisions in the back of the ATV to last them for a week, and if they ran out of drinking water they could boil some river water.

They spent their days exploring the country along the riverbanks. Sens noticed that Meg seemed to know a lot about the various plants around their campsite and she mentioned her dad had encouraged her to manage their garden in Cobar. "After Mum died I wanted to change it so it needed much less watering with the native species I introduced," she said. "You might not have noticed but it's quite big about 0.4 of a hectare in area, plenty of room to keep me busy. Dad loved it too and sometimes came with me to nurseries. I also chatted to some of the

Elders in our area for advice about which ones would be easiest to get going or produce edible bush tucker."

Meg had even persuaded Sens to go skinny dipping with her, when she announced one morning, "Sens you badly need a wash if you want to go on being my friend."

The river was low because there had been little rainfall for the past few seasons, and they found it easy to paddle from their side of the river to the opposite side. Marshall would frantically paddle after them and shake himself all over them as they emerged onto a sandbank and rested in the hot sun.

"You have made me feel young again," Sens remarked. "You have no idea what it's been like having that presence there all the time. I haven't heard from the Nest since we've been here, and I wish they would leave me and Marshall alone."

"I must admit, when you first told me about your dog and the Nest, I simply didn't know what to say. But then there are plenty of mysteries around us which are equally inexplicable," she continued.

"Maybe the Nest can see that we are happy together and has been kind enough to leave us alone."

"Maybe they have, but I have this uneasy feeling that it will not be long before they're back. They have plans which they haven't shared, or for that matter why they needed to communicate with us at all. There must be a reason." Sens thought out loud.

« »

Sens and Meg emerged from their tent at dawn woken by Marshall, who was barking furiously and had charged off down the track. Sens got to his feet to see an ancient 4-WD had appeared and a young couple were getting out. They seemed unfazed by Marshall's watchdog antics, and within a few moments had made friends and given him a biscuit.

Sens wandered over and was about to introduce himself when the young woman put up her hand, signaling for him to stop. "You haven't got your face mask on," she said. "We could be infected and so could you, for that matter. We have just come from Sydney and you know how bad things are there."

She disappeared to the back of the vehicle and scrabbled around, before coming back wearing a face mask. She was holding a spare and offered it to Sens. "My name's Marcia, and that's Tom," she said. Tom was busy pulling bits of camping gear out of the back of their ancient 4-WD and waved a hand at Sens. Marshall seemed to be taking a particular interest in Tom, but then loped back to Sens and sat down next to him.

"Do you have any news from Sydney?" asked Sens. "Our holos don't work here. Is there any sign of a vaccine breakthrough yet?"

They both shook their heads. "It's taken us three days to get here," said Marcia. "It took us nearly the whole of the first day just to get past the Blue Mountains; the traffic was so bad. Everyone was panicking. The ATVs were only able to run on stand-by power and that was soon all gone. People were simply abandoning their transport beside the road and hoping to thumb a lift. We took pity on one couple as far as Bathurst and left them there. I'm worried that one of them could have been infected, although we were using our masks all the time that they were in the ATV."

"So how did you make it here, given the power situation?" asked Sens.

"We're lucky. We were only visiting Sydney and have been travelling in this old four-wheel drive. It's all we can afford and it does go just about anywhere. We've even got an extra fuel tank to help us get around the inland. Interestingly enough, now most vehicles are electric there's little demand on the fuel stations and though there aren't many, there are enough places to get diesel because the farmers are still using it in some areas."

"We were over in NSW from Perth when we first heard about the pandemic in a motel we were staying in. They were warning everyone to stay indoors and not try to go anywhere, but of course huge numbers of people tried to get out of Sydney. There were roadblocks extending out to beyond the Blue Mountains as we were leaving, but we think it was far too late to be effective at stopping the spread of the virus."

"All I know," said Sens, "is that it seems to be a mysterious contagion affecting everyone."

"That's right," said Marcia, "while we were only small kids then, I reckon its much worse than even the COVID-19 virus that happened decades ago."

"What's your understanding of how this disease came about?" asked Sens, interested to hear what the popular media and rumors were saying.

"No one seems to know," said Marcia. "This disease is being reported everywhere. The most common theory is that it is the work of terrorists," she said. "But there are a few loonies who are suggesting that it's extra-terrestrials."

"Oh! That's interesting," said Sens, "and what do they base that on?"

"There are rumors flying around that people and animals have been abducted by flying saucers. Loonies, as I said! You know the type, don't you? We've heard it all before."

"I guess I'd buy the terrorist explanation," said Sens. "It seems more likely to me than coming up with the more outlandish theory of aliens. And we know what the terrorists are capable of, don't we?"

Sens, said the Nest interrupting their pointless discussion, *I must warn you not to stay too close to Tom. Marshall can smell that he has something very wrong with him. I think he might be infected. Make an excuse and tell Meg not to go near them either. I suggest that you should leave without delay.*

As it turned out it was not necessary to make any excuses, because Meg had listened to the discussion between Sens and Marcia about the level of contagion. She was immediately worried about what might be happening to her dad Raegan and thought they should risk going back. They bundled their things into Sens' old

ATV and headed back along the track. Meg had invited Tom and Marcia to come and visit them if they were passing, but no one really believed that they would ever see each other again.

« »

On the long drive back to Cobar, Sens could not resist taking hold of Meg's hand and squeezing it gently.

"Has it been a long time?" she asked him.

"Since I had a Girlfriend you mean?"

"If you want to call it that?"

"It's nice…and, yes, it has been a very long time. It's just Marshall and me these days…and until recently I've been fairly content with my life."

"But that's all changed hasn't it?"

"It's scary, and I don't feel I'm in control of my life any longer. Having you around is really helping me to deal with what's been happening with Marshall. But I can't do what I probably should have…"

Meg shifted her hand to hug his shoulder. "I loved sharing the tent with you even though we were in separate sleeping bags!" she laughed. "But we're going to have to deal with that snoring!"

"That was Marshall!" Sens protested.

"Pull the other one!" Meg paused, and Sens stared along the road with a contented smile on his face, without saying anything.

But Sens could see that Meg had something else to say. "I want to tell you a bit more about me, so it's all out in the open before we take us to a further level."

"Have you got a police record or something worse?" Sens asked with a smile.

"No. I *am* known to the police, but not because I've been convicted of any crime. I'll get to that in a minute. But, of course, my being an Aboriginal Australian has not exactly helped my relationship with the police, as you can imagine."

"Tell me about your mother. Was Irene Aboriginal Australian as well? I've never actually met her."

"No, that's not it. Irene wasn't my mother. She and Raegan first fostered then adopted me when I was about three. My birth mother died soon after I was born, and my Aboriginal father was never around or took any responsibility for me as far as I know. He might even be still alive, but I don't really care, Raegan's always been my Dad. But he's never discussed what he knows of my birth mother or father."

"Maybe it's time to ask?"

"Maybe it is. But there are some things we've avoided ever since I can remember including my adoption, except that once when I was starting school, he told me to say if I was asked that I was adopted and left it at that. But there is something else I want you to know, several things in fact."

"We've all got history you know. Are you sure you want to go on with this, so soon after we've met each other?"

"Yes, it's better you hear it from me." She paused to take a deep breath.

"When I was much younger I was in love with this guy called Damien. He was a really smart guy—a young scientist. He worked in a top-secret research lab on highly confidential projects and never explained what he was doing there. Anyway, one night we'd been at a dance in the bush some distance from Cobar on someone's property and were driving back home. We were giving a friend of Damien's a lift as well. Then, halfway home, this maniac in a four-wheel drive came at us on the wrong side of the road. Damien swerved and rolled the ATV. He died on the scene and his friend was badly injured, but I survived with no lasting injuries, just some bad bruises and headaches which lasted a while. But the memory's never gone away, that's for sure."

"That's how you're known to the police, then?"

"Yes, but there is more to the story. It turned out that the driver who caused the accident was John Williams, the same person we watched opening the Muldoon Estate. He was taken to court for reckless driving causing the death of Damien but managed to get off through lack of direct evidence. It was clear that he had done it but he or his family must have had powerful friends to not get convicted. Ever since then I have done everything in my power to get even with him for what he did."

"It explains your Cobarbarians and the article you wrote in the *Examiner*? And the police obviously know about this? And that's why you've supported us hiding out for a while?"

Meg nodded but her attention was elsewhere. Sens took his eyes off the road for a moment to look at Meg, who had paused mid-sentence. Then he spotted what she was seeing—a line of cars some distance ahead. As they drew closer, they watched police wearing protective masks and coveralls flagging down all vehicles. They were requiring all travelers to stay in their vehicles with their windows closed, scanning identity details through windscreens and turning back anyone who was travelling without an interstate permit.

The man who was checking Sens' ATV looked intently at him and Meg, paying special attention to Marshall on the back seat, and the ATV's registration plate. He then told Sens to proceed to the next checkpoint 500 meters farther down the road, and wait. He refused to explain why.

Later, they were bundled into a paddy wagon waiting to drive them in the opposite direction back towards Bourke, and then beyond Bourke to the razor-wire perimeter of the UFODD Headquarters.

As they were travelling huddled together on the bench in the back of the paddy wagon, Sens comforted Meg. "I don't mind if you tell them everything I've explained about me and Marshall. I'm intending to tell them the truth so it's best to keep out stories straight."

"You may be right, but you have to expect they won't believe us. The police are straight up and down."

"What you don't know is that I was interviewed a while back by two agents who seemed to know a lot about UFOs. So they will probably be involved again, I hope so. They seemed pretty smart and more likely to understand our story than normal detectives." Sens paused. "But whatever happens to us you know that you can count on me don't you? You really mean a lot and I'm hoping that after all this is over we've still got a future." he said.

Meg nodded. "Me too, I feel just the same. And I won't let you down."

No sooner than she had said this they could feel their paddy wagon slowing to a stop and hearing their driver talking with someone. Then there was the sound of a heavy gate clanking open and the wagon starting off again. They both held hands as they felt the noose tighten around them.

CHAPTER 17 Sens and Meg interrogation

At a hastily arranged situation briefing, the UFODD investigations room was abuzz. The double-sided display board based on Sam and Byron's position statement was a jumble of hastily and unresolved felt pen scrawls mud-maps and annotations. They revealed a growing complexity in the situation, with many questions and a few tentative answers, attempting to distil the evidence into a series of relationships between the people and the events. The diagram identified the main players of interest as Sens, his dog Marshall and his apparently new accomplice Meg. Secondary players were Stephen Kay, the journalist at the *Nyngan Examiner*, and other unidentified members of the Cobarbarians.

The role of Meg's father Raegan was unclear. Senator John Williams was also included to one side of the diagram with a big question mark. The relationships between each of the players and the events with which they seemed to be connected were shown as lines. The diagram clarified UFODD's scope of the investigation and also highlighted, despite more than a week of concentrated effort, how little they so far had achieved. After the Muldoon abductions there had been a new impetus to understand what was going on, but as time passed, nothing more substantial had come up.

The first news of Sens and Meg's arrest came directly to Sam via the liaison officer at Bourke Police. She listened intently. "At last!" she said. "Just send them over," and put the phone down. She got up from her chair and did a little war-dance.

Rodney Jensen

"What are you on this morning?" asked Byron.

"The police have just intercepted Sens, his dog, and Meg as well at a roadblock between Louth and Wilcannia. They were recognized by someone who had his wits about him enough to recall that they were on the wanted list we sent out two weeks ago. They should be here very soon," she said triumphantly.

« »

Once inside UFODD, the three were separated. Marshall was left out in a high-walled yard with a hastily contrived shelter, dog food and a bowl of water. Meg and Sens were led to separate cubicles where they were strip-searched, then put through various antiviral procedures, including prolonged hot showers and irradiation with UV, before finally given new white overalls. Their possessions had been tagged and bagged at the reception area and their original clothes incinerated.

They were then escorted to secure holding cells. These contained minimal furniture and were devoid of decoration or color. They relied entirely on harsh artificial light that was never switched off. The rooms were pressurized and capable of being filled with different gas mixtures that conceivably might suit the needs of extra-terrestrials.

Food and water were delivered via a locked and recessed enclosure that signaled content had arrived via a pictogram. A stainless steel toilet and sink combo lay within clear view of a hidden camera. There was a video screen on one wall with which the guards could communicate with their captives, but the screens remained blank for the next twelve hours.

It all formed part of a surreal and calculated strategy to weaken the resolve of enemy aliens who had been trained to withstand the psychological deconstruction and inevitable interrogation that was to come. The process had been borrowed from *UFODD Security Manual 1.0.1.- 'achieving positive interrogation outcomes'*, naively based on the assumption that an alien would think, behave and react in a human-like manner.

Sens' reaction was to stretch out on the hard bed and try to sleep. His first and primary worry was what would become of Marshall, the unfortunate victim of possession. What would happen to him if his captors became convinced that he was the alien? His thoughts turned to Meg, now involved in Sens and Marshall's alien encounters without realizing the dangerous path she had chosen.

It suddenly hit him how angry this all made him feel. He realized suddenly that his feelings for Meg had become a new priority. He was angry that he had needlessly involved her in his problems. But their brief interlude camping beside the Darling River had turned into something far more.

Sens now felt overwhelmed with feelings that he wanted to spend the rest of his life with her. In recent times she and nobody else had made him feel alive and loved. The thought of her counteracted the awful loneliness of his cell. He admired her boldness and her straightforward strength of character in the face of everything that life had thrown her way. He lay on the bed hoping that he would still have the chance to tell her how he felt, now feeling confident that she would reciprocate his feelings.

« »

Sam and Byron had the responsibility of conducting the interrogations of Sens and Meg. They were held in another slightly larger room, also devoid of natural light, and furnished only with a simple table and three chairs. The table held a recording monitor, a flask of water and plastic cups.

In order to reduce the risk of contagion, a plexi-glass screen separated the interrogators from their subjects. Sens was the first to be escorted in by a bored-looking guard in full protective clothing. Appearing far older than his real age, he had dark shadows under his eyes and unkempt hair. He was wearing handcuffs and an expression like he was facing a firing squad.

"You can take those off," said Sam to the guard, pointing at his bound wrists. The guard looked at her questioningly, but she stood her ground. "And then you can wait outside until you're called," she continued.

"Ma'am, that's not protocol," he said anxiously.

"Just do it," she said.

Shaking his head in disapproval, the guard removed the handcuffs and left the room. Sens sat down and took a sip of water with visibly shaking fingers.

Sam explained to Sens that due to the treaty arrangement between the Australian Government and

UFODD, the rights of detainees were not those of citizens subject to Australian law. She went on into a lengthy explanation of the differences, and Sens began to grow impatient.

"So, what it boils down to is that I have no right to legal representation, I am bound to answer truthfully anything you put to me whether or not it might be self-incriminating, and what becomes of me is entirely a matter for you to decide?" he interrupted.

"You got it," said Byron unhelpfully. "But I will say this, Sir. We're pretty good at telling the difference between truth and lies, and it will definitely benefit you to be straight with us. Do we understand each other?" Sens nodded wearily.

Sam glanced at her scribble pad and began the examination.

"So we meet again, Mr. Petersen, under quite similar circumstances, wouldn't you say?"

"I'm not with you," Sens said flatly.

"Let me remind you of the last time we spoke—we of course have this on record. On that occasion you were unable to explain how your dog Marshall and yourself might be connected with the appearance of a UFO above a pet store in Wirrabera, and the disappearance of some puppies on sale in the store. Remember that?"

Sens nodded.

"For the benefit of the record, we require you to answer our questions verbally."

"Yes, I remember that," said Sens.

"On this occasion we'd like you to explain the involvement of you and your dog in the disappearance of Senator John Williams at the opening of the Muldoon Estate, also involving a UFO. You and the dog were there were you not?"

"Yes, we were there," Sens replied heavily.

"Can you explain the disappearance of Senator Williams at the opening?"

"No, I cannot."

"I'd now like to take you back to the time you spent in Bourke Hospital, where according to our records you were suffering from tick bite?"

"So I was told," answered Sens.

"The doctor looking after you mentioned that you believed your dog was responsible for calling the ambulance. Just what did you mean by that?"

"As I explained to him at the time, I expected that Marshall may have attracted attention by standing around in the road," said Sens.

"There is absolutely no evidence of anything like that taking place, either by the communications center that took the call, or by the ambulance team that picked you up. Their report states that they found you unconscious in your ATV, entirely by yourself," said Sam.

"Maybe the people who called the ambulance couldn't wait—I don't know what happened," said Sens.

"We know you're hiding something," said Byron. "You're asking us to believe that someone who went to the trouble of contacting an ambulance would have just left you there unconscious? The fact is, Mr. Petersen, that you believed your dog was somehow responsible for calling the ambulance. That's so, isn't it?" Sens remained silent.

"Since you're unwilling to answer this, it strongly suggests to me that you have something to hide." Sam remarked. Sens started to protest but she put her hand up.

"Let's move on before you dig yourself into an even deeper hole."

She paused to reflect a few moments, working out the best approach to deal with him. "Mr. Petersen," she began again. "You are probably thinking that we would find your notion that Marshall is possessed by an alien intelligence can only mean you are suffering from some form of serious delusion—that's correct, isn't it?" Sens stared at her without answering.

"But the fact of the matter is that we're not what you might think we are—an organization simply tasked with intelligence gathering and suppression of terrorist activity and alien incursion. We were actually set up to deal with cases where people have made sightings of unidentified space craft, people who have claimed to have been abducted, and people who strongly believe that the government has covered up cases of previous encounters such as the Roswell incidents in USA, stories which stubbornly refuse to go away. And then there are other cases similar to yours, where certain people have reported cases of alien possession."

Sens nodded, signaling that he understood her.

"So, let's get back to Marshall," she continued. "Firstly, we have a dog who, despite what you are saying, you genuinely believed capable of calling an ambulance. But this isn't the only amazing ability he has, is it? It has been independently reported that he can do stuff which can only be explained by possession of some intelligence other than dog. He doesn't only talk to you, but he talks to other dogs and animals including sheep and gives them instructions, which they follow, doesn't he?" Sens remained silent again.

"Matt Howard, the property owner who acquired Marshall from the Bourke dog pound, the man whose property you entered without authorization, and the one who you took Marshall back from without permission, told us that Marshall has skills completely beyond any other sheep dog he had come across," she said. "And then there's the evidence we have collated from many people who attended the Muldoon opening who noticed how your dog was able to line up a pack of strays and lead them around the dais like no earthly dog would have been capable of. How do you explain these examples of amazing abilities that no normal dog could possess?"

The two interrogators stared stonily at Sens, watching and waiting for signs that he was about to crack.

"What's going to happen to him?" Sens said at last in a shaky voice.

"That depends on whoever is calling the shots. If you care to enlighten us on that score, we might be able to help," Sam said.

Sens could see that whatever he could say would make little difference so far as Marshall was concerned. He had no idea of what lay in store for him but suspected the worst. His own future was a lesser concern, but maybe if what Sam had just told him, that they were experiencing similar cases of alien possession, was true, then they might be more interested in protecting Marshall than not. So, Sens at last began to explain how he had first heard a voice via Marshall when he had been living on the Mid Coast, a voice he began to call 'the Nest'; how the trip to Cobar via Bourke had been the Nest's suggestion; and how the alien network comprising the Nest had an undisclosed interest in Senator Williams.

"Wow, that's quite a story," said Byron. "Why did you hole up somewhere in the bush instead of letting us know what's been going on? You could have gone to the police, at the very least."

"It's not like that at all," protested Sens. "I could not imagine that the police would believe any of this, or anyone else for that matter."

"Hmm, he's got a point there," said Byron turning to Sam.

She nodded at Byron and decided to try a different approach with Sens. "So from now on we want you to assume that we are not disbelieving what this Nest has been telling you. It is really important for us to try to understand why the Nest has established this communication link and what their plans are."

Sens thought for several moments. "They've been monitoring this planet for a long time and see it as a possible base for their own uses. I am unsure why they should have chosen Earth since they are concerned about many things we humans have done having long term effects on the environment and intend to force us to change our ways."

"Have they explained why they have abducted animals, Senator Williams and his minder," Byron asked.

"Not really but I think it may be connected with the pandemic."

"Have they said anything to make you think that the Nest might have caused it?"

"No, I think it's as much a concern to them as the human activities which are causing climate change and species loss."

"And you believe that?"

"Yes, I have no reason not to."

"Does it worry you that they obviously have the technology and knowledge to effectively make us their slaves?" asked Sam.

"Of course it does. There have been several occasions when they refused to discuss things or answer my questions making me feel that they were not being entirely open about what their plans are and how that might affect us."

"Are they monitoring you and Marshall all the time, including this interview?" asked Byron.

"I think so," said Sens, "I only have to think a question and they usually respond immediately."

"Would you ask them if there is anything that they want to tell us or correct what you have told us?"

Sens was silent for a few moments and had a distracted look as though he was indeed listening to someone else. Finally he looked up. "They said that they intend to talk to you but have not yet decided when that will be."

"What are we going to do with him?" Byron turned to Sam.

"Let's take a break," she said.

« »

With Sens back in his cell, Sam and Byron shared notes from the interview.

"The thing that still puzzles me is why the aliens abducted Williams?" said Byron.

"You know what I think?" said Byron, and continued without waiting for an answer. "We've got to bring that dog back into the cells with Peterson immediately. I think it would encourage him to be even more open with us if he thinks that his dog is safe."

"What are we waiting for? You're right I should have thought of that!" Sam exclaimed, already heading for the yard where Marshall had been temporarily quartered.

When they arrived, there was no sign of Marshall. They searched under the sheltered area and every centimeter of the yard, which was basically bare of anything and surrounded by a high wall. Nothing.

"There's no way he could have climbed or jumped over that wall unless he's sprouted wings," commented Byron. "Where's Cumbrio?"

"Cumbrio?" Sam repeated.

"Yeah, the man who's supposed to be looking after him," said Byron.

They checked with the other guards, and one of them suggested that Cumbrio might have taken Marshall for a walk. "The last time we saw him was about two hours ago," he said. "But he should've been back by now," he continued, frowning.

Byron's attention was elsewhere; he was staring at the sky above them. "Take a look behind you," he murmured to Sam. A black cigar-shaped craft, similar to the ones reported in Wirrabera, South-East Queensland and the Muldoon Estate, had appeared out of nowhere. It looked quite close above them, but they could make out no details on its hull, and it was completely silent. A brilliant cone of light suddenly projected down onto the ground some distance from where they were standing. In a matter of seconds, the cone of light vanished, and the craft was gone before they had time to register what had happened.

"I don't like our chances of finding Cumbrio and that dog," said Sam.

« »

There was little that Sam and Byron could do but wait for a search party to confirm that Cumbrio and Marshall were gone. If the guard and Marshall had ventured too close to the security fence encircling the base, automatic sensors would have been activated, but no alarms had been heard. That at least limited the area to cover, and within an hour the search detail could only conclude that Cumbrio and Marshall had vanished without trace.

Sam and Byron decided that their report of what had happened should wait until they had questioned Meg and determined how well her story corroborated what Sens had been telling them. This time it was Byron's turn to lead the interview.

"Meg, I'm assuming you don't mind me calling you by your first name. Our intention is to keep this interview as informal as possible?" Meg nodded but her body was tense and she was holding her hands locked together on the table.

"Can you first of all explain the nature of your relationship with Sens Petersen?"

Meg reflected for several moments before answering. "I'm not sure what he's told you. We haven't known each other very long but let's just say we have become very good friends. Sens is actually a first cousin of my adoptive father and that was how I met him."

"You know him well enough to have been camping together and long enough to understand what's really going on?" Sam commented.

"I don't know exactly what you mean."

"We think you do," said Sam. "You were at the opening of the Muldoon Estate and witnessed the incident in which Senator Williams, his minder and a pack of dogs were abducted by a UFO. And then you went into hiding together. Why did you do that?"

Meg closed her eyes and sighed, thinking what to say. "There were several reasons. First I thought that my family and Sens would come to the attention of the police or authorities like this one. And Sens' dog would attract similar attention because of his unusual powers over other dogs. He could even end up being experimented on. Secondly, there were several friends of mine from around Cobar at the opening. They are well aware that I am not a fan of the Senator in terms of his politics and corrupt dealings and therefore they might have believed I had something to do with the abduction. And finally, I wanted us to distance myself from my Dad because he didn't understand what was going on either."

"Well just what was going on?" Byron was growing irritated by Meg's unexpectedly smooth handling of her interview. "Can you explain, then, why you and the *Nyngan Examiner* have gone to so much trouble to discredit Senator Williams?"

"Because I have many reasons to utterly despise the man."

"At last, we're getting somewhere," said Byron. "It would help us if you can explain that."

Meg was beginning to realize that her interrogators knew far more than they were letting on.

"Apart from his politics and corrupt involvement in the funding of the Muldoon Estate, my main reason is that he caused the death of a boyfriend I was with in a road accident."

"What lead you to think such a thing?"

"Because I was there in the back of the car Damien was driving. Williams literally forced Damien off the road to avoid a head-on collision. Then there was the hearing where some of the evidence was held in camera. Damien never would tell me what his work was but it was obviously sensitive and I think that was the reason for the hearing to remain closed to the public. One thing I also learned was that there was no evidence that Williams had any alcohol in his bloodstream at the time of the accident. It was something that was reported in the Nyngan Examiner."

Sam and Byron called a halt to the interview and discussed what they'd learned over coffee in UFODD's cafeteria.

"I'm getting the feeling that Petersen and Oswald are almost as much in the dark about the Nest's intentions as we are," said Sam.

Rodney Jensen

"I agree. Now that Petersen has admitted he has been in communication with the Nest and can possibly act as an intermediary between us and the Nest, I think we might be better off turning them loose with security bracelets on. If it were me I'd accept such a deal," said Byron.

"Sens probably would but I'm not sure Graves would agree to it. Let's see what he thinks?"

CHAPTER 18 UFODD Review

The UFODD base close to Bourke was in better shape than many others in the global network. Strict controls over who could come and go and procedures to decontaminate any visitors had so far ensured that there were no cases of infection within the complex, while many other bases internationally had been forced to close down or decamp to safer locations. But everyone on the base was under mounting stress and wondering how long they might be able to maintain their containment lines. Graves not only had to worry about attending to immediate sighting inquiries but was deliberating about what he and his team should do in the worst-case scenario, in which the security fences were breached and the base became untenable.

He'd arranged a global hook-up to assess the status of the pandemic and what possible measures might be taken to assist in the mounting crisis. For many staff of UFODD, remembering 2019, there was a sense of disbelief that a killer pandemic was happening again in USA. Most cities of any size had fatalities in the millions. Whole neighborhoods were barricaded off as 'no-go' areas and the main centers of infection were left for those who were either too poor, or physically incapable of leaving.

Reports within Australia were also concerning, with mounting fatalities matching statistics that had been reached during the COVID 19 crisis more than a decade earlier. Australia's island status meant that the crisis while bad enough was much less than other countries. Mass migrations to regional centers had led to some temporary quarantine camps being established, but the camps were poorly managed and little better than the places that had been left behind. Slightly better off were those in remote places, mostly farmers and graziers used to being self-sufficient for food and water supplies over long periods of time. Their greatest problem was to safeguard their supplies from unwelcome travelers and campers, who were almost impossible to control when it came to stealing stock or other provisions. Many homesteads had become mini-fortresses in which armed family members shared turns at keeping twenty four hour watches over their inner property lines. Patrolling the wider boundaries was done only in a protective posse of fellow landowners, and then only as an absolute necessity, to protect their sheep and cattle from being culled by unwelcome marauders.

As the host for the day, Graves had the responsibility for summarizing the information that had already been circulated and putting forward suggestions for future action. "Fellow delegates," he began in a somber tone. "I would like to share with you some thoughts on this situation in the light of what we have just heard. It may well be that you are of like mind, because the facts leave very few options. Without an immediate fix, our civilization is under the gravest threat imaginable. This disease has traversed every boundary and affected nearly all countries around the world. It is no respecter of authority and our futile attempts to maintain law and order have diminished and are now beyond our resources to manage effectively in many places."

"Our UFODD manpower," he continued, "is rapidly being whittled away, despite our best efforts to maintain stringent protection and isolation practices. And despite our efforts to cordon off the worst affected areas, it is becoming increasingly obvious that badly affected areas now outweigh those that are free of infection. Clearly regions free of infection will not remain that way— we simply have to face the fact that we cannot preserve their integrity for much longer. Before I continue, I would like to hear whether any of you have thoughts to share?"

There was an awkward silence, finally broken by deeply accented tones and peculiar English intonation of UFODD Director of India's Base in Delhi, Kamar Elmaskar. "I would not be wanting to put the cart before the horse, but may I be so bold to suggest that we have all been ignoring the real elephant in this room."

No one responded directly to this observation, but many agitated conversations and murmurings could be heard between the speakers and their advisers.

"I think I know exactly where you are coming from," said Graves finally, "By 'elephant', I presume you are referring to possible extra-terrestrial involvement in this pandemic?"

There was immediate chatter, signaling that most of the delegates were thinking that *was* the case, but Graves was prepared for the question. "We've had the opportunity to investigate in detail recent UFO sightings in this locality. We have also conducted research into possible sources of the pandemic's strain of virus. I am going to invite one of our top agents, Sam Mitchell, who has been involved in these investigations and has the benefit of a scientific background to fill you in on our findings."

Rodney Jensen

Sam and Byron had been given the unenviable task of collating what had so far been discovered about the virus from various international labs still on the UFODD communication net. Sam was also clear about the recent sightings that she and Byron had reviewed. She took the floor and started hesitantly, embarrassed by the elevated status Graves had given her. What on earth was she to say to this assembled group of some of the best brains in the business, most of whom she had never met before face to face like this? She took a deep breath, and plunged in at the deep end

"I would say that there is no evidence that there has been extra-terrestrial involvement in the current pandemic. What we have observed, is the possibility that the extra-terrestrials have been abducting animals in order to work out the degree to which they might be vectors of the disease. We also know that in Australia the virus is a derivative or mutation from the HRNX-0 family, originally developed in clandestine research laboratories both here in Australia and in the United States. HRNX is related to the same virus as rabies, which is carried by fruit bats in some parts of Australia—the virus belongs to the class of viruses called *Lyssavirus*. Unfortunately the new pandemic is caused by a mutation which does not respond to the vaccines which have been used to prevent rabies. It also no longer requires transmission via broken skin but can be transmitted by aerosol infection. That is why this mutation is so deadly."

"Can you tell us where we are at with the latest immunization research?" asked a questioner who was based in the London's UFODD HQ.

"Lyssa has been around for a very long time and is endemic in many parts of the world including Indonesia and parts of Europe. It would appear that we are still some way from finding a breakthrough with this current strain."

"I am generally aware of all that," said Graves, "but what we want to know is what has changed—why do you think it has nothing to do with the UFO sightings?"

"I am in a difficult position here," said Sam. "From what I have seen there is no evidence to support that the new virus is anything more than a version of the original *Lyssavirus*. Its origins are therefore terrestrial rather than extra-terrestrial. Most of the epidemiologists have been saying that the likelihood of fresh global pandemics is not a question of 'whether' but 'when'. Perhaps the most well-known examples of this are the influenza type viruses of the past which in their most virulent form wiped out millions of…"

It was now someone else's turn to interject. "My name's Tom Stanley and I'm based in a remote facility in the Western Highlands of Scotland. "I'm wondering why should you be so confident that this is not connected with the UFOs, considering that they have been abducting dogs and bats, according to your recent investigations?"

"In our view they simply are not connected," said Byron. "We came across horses infected with lyssavirus. We met the vet who was trying to save their lives. In all probability the infection came from a colony of fruit bats in the trees nearby. The night before we had this talk, he told us that some of those same bats were abducted by what appeared to be an alien craft. It could be possible that the aliens wanted to analyze the disease the bats were carrying. That is not to say they were responsible for it," Byron explained. Sam nodded, grateful for his intervention.

At this point Graves took over. "We should remember that germ warfare has been with us since the 20th Century and despite global treaties banning it, has continued to the present day. Even a fairly basic lab can make some of the really dangerous agents—and it's far easier to accomplish that than make a suitcase nuclear bomb, for example. Why raise the alien explanation for the origins of this strain of virus when the most obvious one is terrorists at work? One of the most likely players we've discussed internally is the organization known as Final Solution, but our evidence for that is still circumstantial. In any case, whether it's the work of aliens or crazies, the issues are the same," he said.

"And they are?" Stanley asked.

"Firstly, what measures we should we be taking to contain the virus, and secondly, what can be done to treat those who are infected by it. These are both hugely problematic given the extent of its spread. None of the containment solutions are exactly palatable or practicable. It is, in all probability, too late to contain those who are infected—since they already outnumber those who are not. Various international research sources are showing that containment inevitably fails and developing a vaccine is the best goal. But history has also shown us that it can take years to develop an effective vaccine, by which time…"

"The fact of the matter, without putting too fine a point on it, is that the survival of a base like this may be one of the few chances left for us to get through this crisis." Graves paused to let his summation sink in before continuing. "I think it's time to put our emergency plan into action," he said.

By now he had their full attention, and the silence was palpable.

"The situation here is complicated by the fact that there *have* been a series of confirmed UFO sightings and some abductions. These all appear to be connected with the current pandemic. While I am in complete agreement with Special Agent Mitchell's assessment of where the strain originally came from, I must also pick up our colleague Kamar's suggestion that we cannot ignore the role of the extra-terrestrials.

"I'd like to suggest two possible scenarios based on discussions we have been having with two individuals we are holding, who have provided us with strong evidence of communication with aliens. Their evidence does back up the probability of some connection with the pandemic."

Graves then spent some time summarizing the Sens/Meg interviews, which had his audience's close attention. "What remains unclear is why should aliens be interested at all?" He paused a moment to allow his question to sink in, before continuing.

"The first scenario is perhaps the most obvious, but possibly the least likely, namely that ET has been busy streamlining the original strain of the virus, hoping to wipe us out."

There was a confused and anxious response to this, with many of the delegates trying to speak at the same time. Graves put up his hand and raised his voice a notch. "But as I said, I have reasons to think that another scenario is more plausible, namely that ET, for reasons which are not entirely clear, are here to monitor the situation and help us through this pandemic."

"And what possible evidence do you have for this, Sir?" the agitated tones of Kamar cut through others' interjections.

"This is, of course, speculative," Graves conceded, "but I suppose from the point of view of an intelligence far superior to ours, there would be more to be gained from having a healthy civilian population subject to established codes of conduct and security than a situation of chaos, anarchy, and no prospect of cooperation whatsoever. Most uninformed members of the public, and this might even include you, will be tempted to point the finger at ET rather than accepting the less palatable fact that Earth's own malicious elements are the real offenders behind the pandemic."

Graves was all fired up, despite the fact that his last sentence had drawn an angry response from his audience. "This brings me to a subject which has been discussed and codified by UFODD over a long time. I'm referring to 'Protocol B'," he continued.

"As you are aware, this protocol was developed originally in the late 20th century when concerted efforts were being made to monitor any sources of extra-terrestrial signals from outer space. The early efforts seem laughably unlikely to have produced results, given the inherent assumption that alien communications from presumably far more sophisticated technologies than ours would still be using radio signals of particular frequencies in the same band as those used by our radio telescopes. But as we all know," he continued, "after nearly fifty years of searching by SETI, nothing has ever proven to have been received from an extra-terrestrial intelligence."

"The real dilemma," he continued, "which we faced then, and still do, was whether we should have been attempting to communicate at all, given the uncertainty of who we might be dealing with, and whether or not the outcomes would be at all beneficial for us. Even more debate raged over whether we should continue passively waiting for signals to arrive, or should we send out any message of our own, in the hope that some alien technology might respond to it. I think of it as sending a *message in a bottle* out to sea, in the very unlikely event that whoever eventually were to receive the message would ever understand it." he said.

"Eventually, a special international committee to refine our policy arrived at the decision that there were more likely downside risks than positive ones from such communications. That committee morphed into UFODD and, until this point, the decision has remained enshrined in our 'Protocol B'. In essence it suggests we should never initiate extra-terrestrial contact and if a message is ever received, any reply must be the subject of rigorous oversight, and sent only if there is international agreement to do so. I fear that the time has come, ladies

and gentlemen, that we may have to revisit 'Protocol B',"
he said.

"Please can you clarify what you mean by this, Sir?"
Kamar's voice now had a challenging tone.

"I mean that we must agree to attempt to
communicate directly with the aliens, since they seem to
have been taking an interest in this pandemic. Normally
we would not know where to begin in attempting to
communicate with them, but in this case we at least have
a starting point," said Graves, "and they might be able to
help us."

CHAPTER 19 Protocol B

The decision to release Sens and Meg came as a surprise to them, until they understood there were to be strings attached.

"It's really about the Nest isn't it?" said Meg, the moment they were out of earshot of their captors.

"Yes," said Sens, "definitely."

Following Graves' stark presentation, the meeting was deadlocked in discussion for nearly two hours over whether breaking Protocol B was the right way to go. Those against were unconvinced that the aliens' interest in the pandemic would in any way benefit humans and feared that the effects of their long-term plans would be no different from virtually every case of terrestrial invasion by superior forces in Earth's history. When the main protagonist, Kamar, railed against colonial oppression by the British never having been in India's National interests, Graves countered that argument with some of the more positive legacies India had experienced, such as the legal system, and of course cricket, at which point everyone could not help laughing.

But it was Grave's sober appreciation of the options that was the final clincher. "What choice have we?" he argued. "Our experts are saying that the probability of developing and implementing any vaccine within the next sixty days is as low as 5%, by which time the world population may never recover—we are looking at nothing less than the extinction of *Homo sapiens,*" he said.

Rodney Jensen

In the end, a show of hands gave a majority vote of one in favor of attempting to open up communication lines with the aliens. It was further agreed that Meg and Sens would be released on condition that they agreed to relay a message to the Nest, if and when contact was restored between Sens and his dog. Graves and his two agents also decided that they should be only released if they were wearing security bracelets that could be monitored at all times. If they wanted to travel further afield than Cobar, or possibly Wirrabera, that could only be made only subject to approval.

"I don't know what they're expecting us to do since we don't have the Nest in contact with us at the moment," said Sens wryly.

"At least we've got each other," said Meg with a smile.

« »

The two were braceleted with wrist monitors and bundled into the back of a modified ATV. They were taken to the police vehicle depot at Bourke where Sens' ATV had been left after their arrest. They transferred the few cartons of food supplies provided by UFODD into the back and set off.

Arriving at the outskirts of Cobar the place seemed deserted. Closer to the center the streets were still empty, and they saw nobody. It seemed like the pandemic was making everyone stay indoors or retreat to somewhere more remote. As they drove up the street where Raegan's house was, they could see that it was in darkness.

They pulled up outside the house. Meg had got out of the car before Sens could stop her. He joined her as she had started peering through the glazed panels in the front door. "Nothing!" Meg said softly. She tried the door and discovered that it was unlocked. As it swung open, they recoiled from the smell of the interior. There were ominous buzzing sounds of blow flies. Meg looked at Sens, her lips compressed to a thin line, her eyes desolate.

"Wait here… I'll go and check," said Sens, giving her a quick hug. "I know where his bedroom is."

He went down the central corridor to the back of the house and gingerly opened the door. The buzzing of flies grew louder, and he gagged at the smell of decay. He pulled a handkerchief from his pocket and tied it over his nose, before taking a closer look at the prone body lying on top of the bed. He could see it was Raegan, eyes wide open, still clothed, as though whatever had happened to him was quick. His shirt was caked in vomit. The clouds of flies swarmed incessantly around his face.

Choking from the smell, Sens freed the sheets beneath Raegan's body and wrapped them over him. He then turned to the window and threw it open. Finally, he went outside to comfort Meg. The two looked at each other without saying much. Meg embraced Sens tightly and wept.

"I think he must've been infected with the virus. It would have taken him very quickly and I doubt whether he suffered very long," Sens tried to comfort her.

"He's the only relative I have. He wasn't that old, either. What shall we do now!" She sobbed.

"Go and make yourself a stiff drink. I can't leave Raegan like this. We may be at risk of infection ourselves unless I deal with him immediately."

He found a pick and shovel in a garden shed and began digging a shallow grave in the backyard. His final job was to haul Reagan's body, rolled up in his bedding, and lower him gently into the grave.

He came back into the lounge to find Meg curled up in the corner of a lounge hugging a large, mostly empty glass of what smelled like whisky. She was staring numbly into space, her cheeks tear stained, her hair a mess. She hardly looked at him as he spoke to her. "Meg, do you want to say a few words before we cover him up?" She thought for a moment, registering what he was asking, then nodded, and followed him out to the backyard. She picked out some plants from a neglected flower bed next to the driveway and dropped them over Reagan's body. Then she pulled herself together and began a short speech.

"Dad, I wish we'd talked more now that you're gone and we no longer have the chance. I know that you loved me, and you're the only Dad I've ever had as far as I'm concerned..." She paused, overcome with her grief, lost for words for several moments. Then she continued with a thought that came to her

"You know I'm not into religion much, but maybe your spirit's around this place now, and I hope you're at peace... Farewell Dad." She clung to Sens briefly, and helped him cover the body with the earth from the mound beside the grave.

The two went inside. Sens returned to Reagan's room to dispose of the mattress and remaining bedding outside behind the garden shed. Meg kept herself busy by opening all the windows to help clear the smell. They both showered and disinfected themselves.

Neither Sens nor Meg could face any food, and they retreated to a sofa in the living room, sitting next to each other, simply holding hands.

Sens was first to break the silence.

"Well, at least we're alive, and sort of free," said Sens, before continuing with something he'd been meaning to say for quite some time. "I just want to tell you how much I admire you and how special you've become to me. There was a time in that dreadful UFODD place— that I wondered whether I'd ever be able to tell you this."

A phantom smile crept into her eyes, and she brushed away her tears. "You're pretty special too. I don't know how I'd have coped without you…I'll be in a better state to talk about this—us—you know—tomorrow, and what are we going to do now? Where are we going to live that's safe?"

"I don't suppose we're going to decide all those things immediately," Sens said, ever the practical one, "but what I want to do before anything else is sort out a few things here and make this place a bit more livable."

Meg kissed Sens gently on his cheek. "Can't we just share a bed tonight and not do anything? We can worry about everything else in the morning."

"Of course," said Sens. "I'm not sure your dad would have approved!" They both laughed.

« »

There was more for them to do than either of them realized. Clearing out volumes of stuff that had accumulated over the years occupied their time for a day or two, but the mental toll was harder to deal with. For Meg, staying in the house inevitably brought back all the memories she had of Raegan, but she knew that much had to be disposed of, before she could start again.

One afternoon as the shadows lengthened and the house grew steadily darker, Sens lit a couple of candles and went out to the garage to rummage for something he'd spotted hidden behind a cupboard. He returned triumphantly, carrying an old kerosene lantern in one hand, and an unopened bottle of wine in the other.

"How could we have missed this!" he said with wry humor, as he lifted the bottle to show Meg. The simple act of resuscitating the lantern and pouring some wine into a couple of glasses did more than lighten the gloom.

Meg, wearing a piece of cotton material to keep her hair out of the way and holding a mop in one hand, was slightly bemused by his change in mood. But the glow of the lantern was strangely comforting. It seemed like a special occasion and Sens took Meg in his arms. He was wanting to share his new sense of optimism that they had somehow turned a corner.

The two embraced awkwardly at first, but then, to Sens' surprise, Meg's grip on his shoulders sent an electric shock through his body, bringing with it powerful feelings that had long remained dormant.

As they were embracing, Sens was the first to hear a scratching noise at the back door. Then Meg noticed it. "What's that?" Sens shook his head indicating he had no idea.

"There it is again," said Meg. Then Sens heard a familiar whimper. He raced to the back door, to find Marshall sitting on the doorstep. Marshall was just as excited to see him, and Sens had to shoosh him down as he started barking and jumping all over the place. As Sens was fending Marshall off, he felt a click on his security bracelet. It had become loose. He shook it and it fell to the floor. Meg joined them at the back door, saw Marshall in surprise and stared at Sens and his bracelet on the floor and held up her wrist to show him. "I've been released too!"

She grabbed Sens by the shoulder and danced around for a few seconds in an exuberant release of energy. Sens let her take the lead, infected by her sense of excitement. Eventually they calmed down, but Sens did not let go of her. "Meg," he said carefully, "I just want to say…"

Oh Sens," she interrupted. "This *is* a special occasion, now that we've got Marshall back and we're free! She took his hand softly. "Let's go to bed," she whispered.

« »

Sens found it hard to get to sleep with Meg in his arms. She had drifted off quickly after their lovemaking and was breathing slowly and rhythmically. Sens' brain was busy with a thousand thoughts. The life in Wirrabera he'd once enjoyed now seemed routine and boring. That was before the Nest invaded his peaceful existence, and now Meg set to change everything again!

It was difficult for him to believe he had left the burnt-out ruins of his home only a few months earlier. But the inconceivable had happened and he was experiencing a new sense of purpose, fuelled by possibilities that he had long forsaken. The intensity of his love for this beautiful and courageous woman sleeping beside him was completely overwhelming. Did they really have a new future in front of them? Was there any chance of survival in a world that was looking like an unending disaster? Questions like this without any obvious conclusion continued to circle inside his head until he finally dozed off.

Over breakfast next morning their sense of optimism had not left them and. Meg was particularly chatty.

"For a very long time I have been so angry with what happened to me when I was growing up," Meg explained at last. "And who knows what the future holds. But I started feeling different since the day I first met you. The anger's gone. The past is past. Having you around has changed all that."

CHAPTER 20 Departure plans

UFODD was abuzz. Commander Graves had issued an in-mail *PRIORITY-MUST READ* note to all staff requiring them to listen in to an internal broadcast he would make the following morning at 0800 hrs.

Byron and Sam speculated what was so urgent as to command all staff attention like this. Could it be something to do with new pandemic protocols? The normal channels of behind the scenes chat were silent. Nobody seemed to have an inkling of what he was about to say.

When Graves came on their screens at the appointed time he was holding himself stiffly, radiating a sense of urgency as if UFODD was under siege. He stared at the camera for a few seconds before clearing his throat and finally began his announcement.

"What I am about to say has been on my mind constantly during the last few days. I have now had the benefit of consulting my colleagues in the United States and liaising with Australian National Government regarding the pandemic situation. None of you could have failed to see the gravity of what has been unfolding, not just in Australia, but around the globe. It is affecting all our supply lines, our sources of energy, our food and water. An installation such as this can function in the short term with what is in storage but not indefinitely. And from my discussions there appears to be not even a glimmer of light in the tunnel. Even on a strict ration regime, we have a maximum of six weeks to hold out here. After that it would be problematic for the 100 or so personnel here to have sufficient resources to survive.

Rodney Jensen

After that it will be almost impossible for staff to find anywhere else in this region that will be safe to live, let alone find employment.

"I have therefore decided that we must vacate within the next 72 hours. Regrettably, those staff who do not hold permanent residency permits for Australia will have their work with us terminated as of this morning. I am making arrangements to transport those of you in this category as soon as you are packed and ready to leave."

"US Citizens among us on temporary visas will be leaving on a special charter flight to Los Angeles. I will be speaking personally to all such staff about this shortly. Please be ready to deploy within 48 hours' notice.

"I can only say that it has been a privilege to work with each and every one of you, and it is with great sadness that I should be making this announcement. Obviously, we are in the midst of a crisis brought on by the pandemic, which has made continuation of this installation impossible. THANK YOU."

Byron and Sam who had been watching the announcement stared at each other mutely. Byron was the first to break the silence.

"I'm not going back. There's nothing for me in the United States, as you know."

"My mum's still at that place where we quarantined after the Blue Mountains," she said. "The Council let her stay on because returning to her own home is not a safe option any longer. We could go there for a bit if you like?

Come to think of it you were talking about buying a property. Did you find any agents to talk to?"

"Yes I've talked to a couple. There are several country properties on the market most much too big for me to manage but one maybe a possibility. I was intending to find time to take a look when things settled down here."

"Where is it? Is it anywhere near here?"

"It's about 50 k's to the east in semi-desert country. Sounds pretty much what I've been looking for. It's got 500 acres of grazing land and wouldn't cost much because it's a deceased estate in a poor state of repair, according to the land-sales agent, and people aren't exactly queuing up to buy. The agent said the owners have been running sheep on it but it needs checking out."

"I wouldn't mind coming with you. I'm no expert on country properties but maybe there are things I'd notice that you could miss."

"That would be great. Truth is I know virtually nothing about being a farmer." Byron paused for a second, looking hesitant, unlike his usual self. "I've been wondering whether you've given any thought about my offer for us to go into partnership? I'd prefer not to do this by myself and as I said before, there'd be no strings attached."

"I didn't think you were that serious when you talked about this before, Byron. What are you asking me? Do you actually know anything about sheep farming? Because I don't, and I'm not really sure I want to become a farmer's partner on a property miles from nowhere!"

"Don't worry, I am not trying to push you into anything. As I said, I have been told about one property that sounds like a possibility. Let's go and check it out and maybe I'll make an offer. We could do worse. What do you think?"

Sam looked bemused. She placed a hand on Byron's forehead and stroked it slightly. "I think Grave's announcement has made you a tiny bit crazy. You don't just start farming with no experience, no machinery and a host of other stuff you'll need quite apart from livestock. Global warming has made anywhere around Bourke completely untenable for conventional farming. I know you're not stupid, but wonder if you have really appreciated the difficulties of such a venture. I might be more interested if you could show me a proper feasibility study. We can't just live on a remote property without any income or supplies!"

Now Byron really did surprise her. He pulled a data chip out of his pocket and handed it to her.

"Here's the broad brush financial assessment you're after. I've been putting this together in my spare time with the help of a retired rural expert I found online. Admittedly the costs and returns are based pretty much on what this consultant, the agents and farmers have told me. And yes there are quite a few assumptions and what you guys call 'rubbery' figures."

"This is worse than I thought! You really are serious about this?"

"I was going to surprise you later on, but Graves made his decision sooner than I was expecting. Please take a look. It's not just off the top of my head. Despite what I've said before about my Dad, one thing he did teach me was how to read a balance sheet, and I do understand how difficult this enterprise will be. But for my money it's better than sitting on our hands."

Sam could see he was sincere and felt that she had underestimated him. *Maybe for once her assumption that simply because she was born here would make her automatically right about everything needed to be revised.*

« »

The place Byron was looking into turned out to be nearly two hour's drive from Bourke at the end of a dusty rutted track. The entrance gate was unlocked, and a small homestead stood about 100m from the road accessed at the end of a narrow gravel driveway. There had been attempts in the past to grow an avenue of trees using stubby eucalypts common to the region, but they looked unattractive and neglected.

They drove up the driveway and parked in a standing area beside the house. They found a short flight of stone steps leading to a wide veranda that encircled the building. The house was all on one level with a steeply pitched iron roof. The roof showed large patches of rust and several sheets had worked loose and were flapping in the wind. The screen door was also banging open and shut annoyingly as the wind caught it.

Byron tried the front door and to his surprise it squeaked open as though the hinges had never been oiled. He peered inside along a central corridor running the width of the interior to a rear door. All the rooms were arranged along both sides of the corridor.

"Bad Feng Shui," murmured Sam. "The Chinese would never live here. They think their luck runs straight through a place like this!"

"Good for cross ventilation, but..." Byron was concentrating on where he should step, noticing that there was a lot of give in the boards and gaps where white ants had eaten their way through in some places.

They checked out all the rooms dodging spider webs and huge ants, almost immediately feeling the itch of flea bites. "There must have been a dog here," Sam said. "The eggs lie dormant and hatch once they feel vibrations."

"Add fumigation to the list," Byron remarked

The back of the house was also unlocked, and they found that they had to jump off the back veranda to the ground below because the stairs were broken.

They didn't spend very long inside the house because Byron was anxious to look at the paddocks. Viewing the home from the rear as they reached the back garden fence, he summed up what they both now realized. "It's much too far gone to fix. Everything would have to be replaced and would cost a fortune to make it comfortable. It would be much cheaper to knock it all down and start again."

"Sad though, I think. It does have an antique charm lurking behind all the dirt and neglect. Don't you think?" said Sam.

"Maybe, but I don't want to spend years renovating a house. I'd prefer to bring in a prefab. It would be far quicker and cheaper in the long run. Can we take a look at the paddocks or whatever you call them now?"

"Yes, but let's drive, it'd be dark before we even begin looking around properly," Sam said.

They drove from one paddock to the next. There were no livestock to be seen and most of the gates had either been left open or had fallen to the ground, their hinges given up to corrosion. Barbed wire fences were in a similar state of decay with posts eaten out by white ant and barbed wire rusted beyond repair.

They discovered one large dam with no water in it. The clay pan was riddled with huge cracks and hoof prints.

The accumulated decay and neglect was something that could conceivably be fixed, but an empty dam in the face of a hostile, rainless climate stretching far out to the future was too much for Sam.

"Byron, you can't still be serious that you want to live here with me, can you?" she said feeling miserable to be giving in rather than accepting it as a challenge.

"I think we would be safer here than anywhere else in the world."

"But at what cost?"

"You'll grow to love it, I'm sure."

"Convince me!"

Rodney Jensen

"How about just a 12-month trial? Think of it as a new adventure."

"You're nuts!"

CHAPTER 21 Sam meets the Nest

With the option to either stay or leave pending further developments, Sam had decided to stay on in UFODD, while Byron was working on convincing her to join him in his farming venture.

When she arrived at her work station after a troubled night wondering what to do with her immediate future she found a priority note on her intra-net. She looked around and found that Byron was already there staring intently at something on his monitor.

"Have you seen this note about Petersen and Oswald?" she asked him.

"Their security bracelets?"

"Yes, they've suddenly managed to de-activate them I see."

"It means that they can go anywhere they want from now on and we won't have a clue. But you know what? I don't think they're the major players."

"For once I agree with you Byron," said Sam as she watched a stream of vehicles departing the complex carrying baggage and other boxed up materials that could not be left behind, were making numerous round trips to Bourke Airport and back. The noise was constant and annoying. Then her holo beeped. She looked at the caller details in surprise, put a finger to her lips to signal Byron to listen in, and pressed *contact* on the screen.

"Mr. Petersen, what a surprise. What can we do for you?"

"Firstly, I was very grateful that our security bracelets were de-activated yesterday, but my purpose in calling is to tell you about a discovery we've made."

"Hmm, what discovery? And just to let you know, I have Agent Lowe with me."

"I think it's better if we meet in person, rather than my explaining this over a holo. Would it be possible for both of you to come to the offices of the Nyngan Examiner with Stephen Kay, who I believe you've already met?"

"Yes, we'll be there, what time?"

The moment she had terminated the call, she turned to Byron. "It must have been ET who de-activated their security bracelets."

"I think you're right again?" she sighed.

« »

Graves had raised an eyebrow about this new development, which given his recent announcement he didn't really want to know about. He was also unaware of any order to release Meg and Sens from their bracelets. After some discussion, he agreed to their meeting, and hoped that it would put a line under their interrogations.

The journey was uneventful, and Nyngan showed few signs of life as they found their way to the *Examiner's* office once again.

Their first surprise was to find the person guarding the door was someone Byron recognized.

"It's Cumbrio, isn't it?"

Cumbrio nodded.

"Well, what happened to you?"

He looked uncomfortable. "I not know exactly. One moment I taking your prisoner dog Marshall for walk, next thing, I outside this office. I see I been out long time," he said tapping his head. "Sun low and I having lunch when I take dog for walk. When I wake here sunset happening. I ask people for help. We get to talk, they say stay! I say yes. So here I am. I not want go back UFODD."

"Wow that's amazing, and you can't remember anything that happened to you between taking the dog out and arriving here? You've been missing for quite some time."

Cumbrio just shook his head. "We go meet Mr. Kay. He waiting for you," he said.

« »

Inside the Examiner's newsroom, Sens, Meg, Byron and Sam were seated with Stephen Kay, looking intently at a display on an ancient pc monitor.

Sam was not keen on small talk and didn't much like Kay, whom she'd felt had been extremely evasive at their last encounter. "I hope whatever this is all about has been worth our coming all this way!"

"Did the Nest explain to you what happened to Marshall?" Byron asked Sens.

"Yes, Marshall was returned to us in Cobar. We've worked out that he was released at about the same time Cumbrio turned up at the offices here."

"And Cumbrio had no recollection of what happened to him, he told us."

"Yes, that's right," said Stephen. "But Cumbrio hasn't been showing any obvious effects on his state of mind as far as we can see."

"Marshall seems unaffected too," said Sens. "But I had another reason for asking you to come here and discuss this in private."

"Sounds like something you want only us to hear?"

"That's right. the Nest wants to talk to you Sam, if you're willing. I thought that it would be better for you to have a conversation with them here, rather than at UFODD?"

"Now I have some reservations," said Sam. "I think it would be better if UFODD were involved. It's the only organization I'm aware of that is geared up for extra-terrestrial communications."

"Oh okay. I see what you mean."

"So all we need to do with your alien messenger is confirm that I'll be ready for a contact tomorrow at UFODD. I am assuming that it won't really affect them where or when it happens. And I'm assuming that Marshall is not required for this communication?"

"That's right. But they also warned that if UFODD was hoping to record the Nest's side of any communications *'it would not work,'* to quote them, because the messages are telepathic rather than electronic."

« »

Sam and Byron managed to catch Commander Grave's attention on their return to base later that day. He seemed strangely distracted despite a unique opportunity to communicate with an extraterrestrial source first-hand.

"I realize that the current focus is on decommissioning UFODD Australia, but you can surely appreciate the significance of this communication?" said Sam.

"The problem I'm having is that we won't gain a great deal from a one-sided conversation."

"I'll be taking detailed notes of everything they say. We cannot miss this opportunity of learning more about their objectives."

Graves pondered for several moments before finally lifting his head and staring directly at her.

"I hope you've been practicing your shorthand. I want every syllable of what they're saying noted. On our part, we'll set you up in the soundproof comms studio and make sure you have everything you say recorded and transcribed, with spaces to include your notes. I'd like the entire conversation in our files before I leave this installation and preferably tomorrow. It must also be given the highest security classification. Only you, Byron and myself shall have access to the files until I say otherwise. Understood?"

"Yessir!"

Sens had sent Sam a text message confirming that the Nest would contact her at 10.00 am the following morning. UFODD arranged for Sam to receive the message in their comms suite with video and audio recorders monitoring everything.

As the digital timer on her table clicked down to zero, she heard the voice inside her head. While it was expected she still felt strangely vulnerable, and unbalanced.

Hello Sam, please do not be alarmed. The voice was softly modulated and female. *You may call me 'Leila'. Please understand it is merely for your convenience that we have chosen this mode of communication.*

"Can you read my thoughts, should I bother speaking?" Sam asked, for the benefit of her observers in the comms room.

We think it might be best if you conduct your own questions and replies verbally. While your colleagues will only hear you, it may help to convince them that this contact is real. We're communicating with you alone because we trust your integrity and must do all we can to minimize the risk of other hostile agents attempting to breach our security. For that reason your colleagues in UFODD will discover that none of your monitoring devices will detect our side of this communication.

"Why have you chosen me?"

You are more useful to us than Sens and Marshall. We originally sought anonymity in our transactions with your people, but the situation has changed. We have also discovered that Marshall has only a matter of months to live. You may or may not wish to share that with Mr. Petersen.

"Why did you abduct people and animals - Senator Williams, UFFOD's Guard Cumbrio, dogs and bats etc.?"

We had our reasons which we need not go into, beyond saying that we have conducted experiments to verify the cause of your pandemic and find a cure if possible. Cumbrio proved very useful, as it happened.

"Oh?" said Sam.

We were able to include him in a trial of a vaccine we have developed to help slow the spread of the pandemic. In his case it has proved completely effective, and his freshly stimulated immune system has resisted all attempts by us to infect him with the virus.

Sam chose to ignore the ruthless efficiency and casual disregard for risk that Leila's Nest employed in its clinical trials. "The people at UFODD want to talk to you more about the pandemic," she said. "Is there anything that your Nest can do to help us?"

Ideally, we would continue our testing to ensure that the long-term effects on human physiology are free of side effects, but we may assist you to fast track your vaccine development given the urgency.

For a few moments, Sam heard nothing and her shorthand scribbles stopped. The others in the comms room looked at each other in consternation wondering if that was all they were going to hear. But then Sam started writing again, and there was an audible sigh of relief.

The main purpose of this conversation is to alert you to a change affecting our territorial management of Earth. We have learnt that our opposing Nest, the Aggressives, have decided to breach our longstanding treaty and ignore our Earth responsibilities. We do not know when their impact will become obvious to you, but we've decided not to intervene directly and escalate hostilities. Instead we will liaise with you over the best means to counter their invasion.

"You cannot be serious. How could Earth muster any effective response to your far greater technology and powers?"

We will have to address that problem once we know more. Meanwhile we will not communicate any further unless we uncover tangible evidence of the Aggressives' plans. That is all we have to say for now. Should you feel the need to contact us in future simply think 'Leila' as though you were calling her to contact you back, and we may or may not respond depending on context and circumstances...

Sam put up her hand to show the conversation was over. For those in the observation room it was a most frustrating experience to have so little inkling or tangible evidence of what was being exchanged. As the Nest had warned, none of the recording devices, except the audio/visual feed of Sam speaking provided any record of the discussion. They only had her side of the conversation and her shorthand notes of what the Nest had to say. Graves was strangely unimpressed or appeared to be, when he excused himself from the meeting explaining he had several urgent matters to deal with waiting for his attention.

"It was the weirdest thing," Sam said to the others. "It was just like the 'the Nest' contact Sens told us of in his interrogation, except there was something very different. The voice I heard was a woman's. She had a definite personality, radiating warmth and insight—it was as though she had known me all my life…"

"Like your mother?" suggested Byron.

"No not exactly—more like an experienced therapist—the sort you could trust and confide in. But of course 'Leila', as the Nest calls itself, is really no different from the Sens' Nest contact. She said that it is just the Nest's way of making us feel comfortable."

"Sounds cozy, but I don't like the way they are keeping us and everyone else but you in the dark," said Byron.

"Bottom line is that the Nest's claim there is another Alien Nest, the 'Aggressives', who if unchecked, are set to annihilate the human race. Leila's Nest wants our help to defeat them. Can we afford to ignore this warning, if it's to be believed, and an even bigger 'if, *are we definitely choosing the right side?*"

"That's anyone's guess, isn't it?" said Byron.

CHAPTER 22 The Trojan Horse

Graves was in the middle of deciding what to keep and what to jettison out of his accumulated physical documents and mementos cluttering his office, when he felt his holo vibrating. The face on the screen seemed slightly familiar but the title convinced him to take the call. It was Sheila Armstrong, from AU Security.

"Sheila, to what do I owe this pleasure. I believe we met at a conference quite a while back?"

"That's right. At the round-table in Canberra 2 years ago. I headed the special committee for UFO sightings on behalf of AuSecurity. I was wondering if I could catch you before you leave our shores?" Sheila asked.

"So, you know about our departure?" Graves was taken aback, because it had not been his intention to broadcast UFODD's departure plans to anyone but a very select list of names. Sheila wasn't on it.

"I do, and in normal circumstances I would not have bothered you, but I need to meet briefly in person if that's possible. Will you be available tomorrow morning? I have arranged special transport to your base and I won't take up much of your time for our discussion."

Graves immediate reaction was to tell her he was much too busy, and in the normal scheme of things he would not have taken much notice of an Australian Government official's request like this. But on reflection, *why create a bad impression of non-cooperation from UFODD? We might even be back some day!*

"OK, I can understand that it must be very serious for you to go to such trouble. How about we make it 9.00 am, and I'll lay on breakfast in our executive lounge."

« »

Sheila was flustered and embarrassed to be arriving nearly one hour later than her appointed time. "The pilot who was meant to be bringing me called in sick at the last minute. I'm terribly sorry."

"It doesn't matter, Sheila," said Graves magnanimously. "Sit down and relax while I order the breakfast I promised. What do you like—continental or the works, bacon, eggs, hash browns, whatever?"

"I must say this is better than QANTAS! Continental's fine, and coffee, that's all."

Sheila quickly sipped her coffee and began sorting through some files on her holo.

"So, what's this about? It must be serious?" Graves asked.

Sheila stopped fumbling with her papers and stared back at him with. "It's the most troubling thing that I've been involved in since I was appointed. I could not discuss this with you on your holo. But I've come here to beg you to reconsider your departure plans."

"That serious?"

"Potentially, yes. I will try to give you the basic points. You can keep copies of a couple of reports on the basis that they are for your eyes only."

Rodney Jensen

"OK let's have it."

"What originally came to our attention was something that happened decades ago. An important discovery was confirmed by one of our agents who worked for the Australian Embassy at the time. He observed an object in the process of being uncovered by troops in Equatorial Sumatra. It was a spherical object which they somehow energized. Some of them disappeared when they pressed the wrong button."

"You mean…?"

"They simply disappeared without trace. And have never been recovered. Indonesia chose to bury the sphere where it lay and try to keep a lid on what had happened. But our agent who had been captured and subsequently deported urged us to see its immense significance."

"The opportunity to find out more arose some years later at the highest level for Australia. Our experts were asked to assist Indonesia, and subject to a special agreement, we sent scientists over to transport the globe to a secure repository here. It was located on the edge of Sydney in a former military base, known as 'Moorebank', where it remained for some time until some of our scientists began taking a much closer look. The conclusion they came to was that it is an alien transporting device that is able to transport things and possibly animate beings to other places in space."

"Uh huh," mumbled Graves, "I can understand the need for secrecy on this. Do I assume that the movement of things and animate beings could equally be incoming?"

"That's precisely our concern. We fear that it's, in effect, a Trojan Horse, which lays our planet open to invasion we can't control. The alarm bells rang when one of our scientists experimenting on the settings of the globe winked himself out of existence. It was almost the same as reported by our agent in Indonesia who saw this happen to the Indonesian soldiers. We immediately put a hold on any further experimentation and shut the Moorebank repository down. Subsequently, we moved the Globe to a remote location in the Simpson Desert, it's known by the Code Name of 'Site 51'.

"And that's not as far from us as it is to Sydney?"

"Correct, that's why I wanted to meet."

"There have been more transport episodes?"

"Yes, but not people. Some agents of ours made an inspection of Site 51 a short while back.

"Was it routine?"

"No, not really. One of our agents was having some strange premonitions that the repository was not as it should be. She could not explain much about these premonitions except to say that they were really like dreams. When she discussed the detail of what she had seen, these premonitions described the repository so accurately that we came to the conclusion she was receiving them from the aliens themselves."

"And your investigators found something untoward?"

"Yes, you could say that. The repository was empty but completely intact and undamaged. The globe had been built in and could not have been moved without the enclosure being totally de-constructed, and there was no evidence that could have been done."

"Sounds like alien hands at work doesn't it? A case of a transporter transporting itself?" Graves remarked.

"Yes. We have no idea where it is now, but suspect it might be setting up a base somewhere else. We desperately need help to find where it is, assuming it is still somewhere on Earth. Would you reconsider your decision to leave? We definitely need your help. Your organization is best equipped to provide it."

"You are putting me in a really difficult position. Most of my staff have already left this installation. I am scheduled to go myself in two days. There will only be a skeleton staff of half a dozen people remaining on a caretaker basis. They are not professional case officers and wouldn't be of any help to you."

"I am authorized to offer you financial compensation for any overheads you would incur by maintaining some presence and providing assistance to us if that might help change your mind?"

"When were you intending to head back to Canberra?"

"Later today."

"I need to give some thought to this. The biggest problem is whether I decide to stay or go myself."

"Do you have immediate family in the States?"

"Yes and no. My children are grown up and I'm divorced, so that's not really my main concern."

"I see," said Sheila, not really understanding him.

"Just give me a few hours and I'll let you know what I've decided before you leave. Meanwhile, I'll ask my secretary to provide you with office space and anything you need."

At the end of the day Graves changed his travel plans so that he could await further developments in the Site 51 mystery and assist as needed.

« »

THE END

EPILOGUE

Everyone at first had high hopes that a new vaccine based on Cumbrio's antibodies would provide immunity to the pandemic, but the trials failed. Cumbrio himself became re-infected by a second wave of the virus, and spent weeks in hospital before eventually recovering. The second wave of the pandemic was even more virulent than the first and ended up infecting most of the human population.

Sens was not content living in the virtual ghost town that Cobar had become as a result of the pandemic. He asked Meg if she would come and make a home together in coastal Wirrabera. As the Nest had predicted, Marshall soon reached the end of his days peacefully. He quietly passed, still dreaming of rounding up sheep.

After much deliberation and negotiation, Byron and Sam decided that they would make a go of improving the property they'd surveyed. They negotiated a *land only* deal with the pastoral agent, had the old homestead removed and purchased a simple prefab. three bedroom home which arrived at the site on the back of an over-wide transport vehicle.

Six months later they were working on the fences, had sunk a bore hole to replenish the dam and had begun importing sheep. The biggest problem they had was lack of reliable rain.

Byron had given up hope that he would ever return to America. Sam, after her first encounter with the extra-terrestrials found it difficult to sleep at night, wondering when or if she would be visited again.

Acknowledgments

During the past decade, gloomy predictions on global pandemic and its far reaching economic social and environmental effects have been fully vindicated by the COVID19 Global Pandemic. This is a comprehensive revision of an earlier novel with the invaluable assistance and advice of Chloe Barber-Hancock. I must also acknowledge the untiring and generous contribution of my partner Liz McCarthy in reviewing and proofing this and previous re-drafts. I also owe a debt of gratitude to various self-publishing gurus including Mark Dawson and David Gaughran.

Please review this novel

I hope that you enjoyed 'Covert Messages'. I would appreciate it if you could spare a few moments to write a sentence or two in review. This helps other readers to decide if it is something they might also enjoy, and also it very much helps me as an author.

Go to Rodney's website to review Covert Messages

https://www.rodneyjensenbooks.com/review-covert-messages/

« »

Be one of the first to read the second volume of the Covert Trilogy

In 'Covert Citadel', you will learn how arch rivals of the Nest, the 'Aggressives', take advantage of the pandemic weakened population of Earth to attempt global conquest of the planet.

Sign up to Rodney Jensen Books Mailing List

https://www.subscribepage.com/y4a2w9_copy2

…. and I will let you know as soon as it is available.

« »

Rodney Jensen

About the author

Rodney Jensen is a speculative fiction writer focused on how current trends will shape the near future. The early version of Covert Messages was written several years before the COVID 19 pandemic. It has been interesting to find that many of his original speculations about global pandemics have proven to be accurate and required only minor revisions in light of recent actual events.

Other aspects of his speculative fiction are influenced by his environmental background, experience as an urban designer and passion for renewable energy. Similarly his interests in artificial intelligence, the search for extra-terrestrial intelligence (SETI) and new theories of the cosmos have been important inspirations.

He is fascinated by the notion of a cosmic-scale artificial intelligence network waiting for the appropriate time to make first contact with humankind. Rodney hopes that within his own lifetime the discovery of extra-terrestrial intelligence will overturn the generally held belief that our intelligent species is alone in the cosmos.

Other Books by Rodney Jensen

Find out more about Rodney, these and other books at his website: http://www.rodneyjensenbooks.com/

Rodney Jensen

What reviewers have said about Rodney Jensen's books ...

"If you enjoy futuristic science fiction and extra-terrestrial experiences, this is the book for you. The references to the past COVID-19 pandemic of 2020 are chilling and force you to consider our own current situation, as the more serious pandemic of 2035 unfolds in the book. Rodney Jensen utilises his knowledge of Australian geography as he weaves a sombre tale, but includes the more positive romance or two as well. Also, I found the antics and behaviour of the dog Marshall as he is unknowingly manipulated by the extra-terrestrials quite delightful." Elizabeth Saadeh

« »

"Much thought, imagination and care has gone into this chilling and provocative novel. It ['Covert Citadel'] is a post -pandemic dystopian vision set in the out-back wastes of New South Wales and its devastated towns where a courageous few eke out a sparse existence. A young woman, Sam Mitchell provides hope, rallying a brave band of technologically adept survivors who stand up to the threat of a sinister and destructive alien power." Jenny Towndrow.

« »

"The novel [now entitled 'Covert State'] is a well-paced traditional detective story set in the near future with a concealed sci-fi twist. The characters are engaging, skilfully presented as people you may already know. It takes you on a journey through Adelaide and its Hills, Sydney and the enigma that is Indonesia and its stormy relationship with Australia. An easy to read and most enjoyable Australian crime novel." Andy McGee.

9 780099 416883